Sting of the Zygons

2/14

DOCTOR·WHO

Sting
of the
Zygons

STEPHEN COLE

BBC
BOOKS

2 4 6 8 10 9 7 5 3 1

First published in 2007 by BBC Books, an imprint of Ebury Publishing.
A Random House Group Company.

This paperback edition published in 2008

Doctor Who is a BBC Wales production for BBC One
Executive Producers: Russell T Davies and Julie Gardner
Series Producer: Phil Collinson

The Random House Group Ltd Reg. No. 954009.

Addresses for companies within the Random House Group can be found at
www.randomhouse.co.uk.

A CIP catalogue record for this book is available from the British Library.

ISBN 978 1849907118

The Random House Group Limited supports The Forest Stewardship
Council® (FSC®), the leading international forest-certification organisation.
Our books carrying the FSC label are printed on FSC®-certified paper.
FSC is the only forest-certification scheme supported by the leading
environmental organisations, including Greenpeace. Our
paper procurement policy can be found at
www.randomhouse.co.uk/environment

Series Consultant: Justin Richards
Project Editor: Steve Tribe
Cover design by Henry Steadman © BBC 2007

Typeset in Albertina and Deviant Strain

Printed and bound in Great Britain by Clays Ltd, St Ives plc

For Justin Richards
And for his 400 Drahvins called Dawn

The beast appeared with a shrieking roar.

Within moments, Bill Farrow's ears were ringing with the screams of villagers, the shattering of slate, the howling of terrified dogs. The hell-creature had smashed straight through the manor house, its scaly head rising up from the wreckage of stone, savage eyes staring round as if hunting for fresh targets. Then the beast moved forwards, crashing through the ancient stone walls like they were chalk, tearing up the flawless lawns and the topiaries Bill had so carefully cut only days before.

The Devil himself's come to judge us, thought Bill fearfully, wishing he'd drunk less and listened more to the vicar's words that morning. He turned, stumbled and ran, spitting snatches of prayer under his breath.

A gang of young men had grabbed pitchforks and scythes and were gathering in the churchyard. They shouted for Bill to join them as he passed. But Bill ran on. Might as well attack the thing with peashooters – the beast's strength was hideous, hell-born. *It can trample stone*, he wanted to shout at the men, *it can level a house with a brush of that tail, you can't stop it.*

But his lips remained set in a grimace of pure terror as he ran and ran. The yowls of children and the cries of women grew a little fainter in his ears, but the image of the beast was burned into his brain in horrible snatches – massive ivory fangs, the black scales packed over its glistening bulk. Bill heard the rending of rock close behind him like the boom of thunder – *It's coming after you* – and ran faster as the creature's hunting roar tore through the air. Bill was heading for the canal. If he got into the water, perhaps this thing would lose his scent…

A tremor thumped through the ground, knocking him off his feet. He fell heavily on the path, palms stinging, knees grazed raw. A blast of hot, sour breath enveloped him as he struggled to rise.

Don't look back, Bill willed himself desperately, but the screams of young men, the wet crush of trampled flesh compelled him to turn.

The beast was towering above him. Its dark eyes stared down. A thick rope of drool splashed over his chest as the terrible jaws snapped open…

And then the monster stopped dead.

Bill stared up at it, tears wetting his cheeks, his breath coming in painful rasps.

The beast's huge, snake-like head had turned to one side as if listening to something. Its bloodshot eyes were glazing over. And a new sound filled Bill's ears.

A rhythmic, whispering, chirruping sound. A sound no creature of God could have made.

Bill craned his neck to see behind him and saw the girl. It was the Meltons' lass, barely eight summers old. Her skin was pale and dirt-streaked, with blonde hair and piercing blue eyes that stared up at the creature, unafraid.

'Get back, Molly,' Bill called hoarsely. 'It's not safe here.'

Only then did he remember the girl had gone missing days ago and not been seen since.

The mighty beast growled, snatching back Bill's attention. He shivered, scrabbled out from beneath its shadow and, as he started towards Molly, saw a slight, well-dressed man push past her.

'Sir Albert!' Bill said hoarsely. 'Sir, we must take Molly and flee for our lives…'

Sir Albert Morton was clutching something in his hand. It was the size of a fir cone, but glistening like wet skin. Bill realised that this was the source of the shivering, whispering sound that seemed to hold the beast transfixed. He regarded his employer warily, the white skin, the unblinking eyes. It was like Sir Albert was under a spell, enchanted.

'Sir?' he said quietly. No reaction. 'For pity's sake, sir!'

He grabbed hold of Morton's free hand and pulled him away. 'We must get away from here!'

But then the towering beast jerked awake from its trance. A spasm wrenched through its neck, and the ground thundered as it blundered away, clearing the canal in a single stride, heading for Lake Kelmore.

'We're saved!' Bill shouted. 'God be praised—'

'You fool!' Morton turned and smacked him away with the back of one hand.

The power in the blow knocked Bill to his knees. How could such a slender man be so strong? What *was* that in Morton's hand? The questions clouded Bill's mind, left him kneeling when every instinct told him to run.

Then it was too late.

Morton's face was changing. A devil-red glow had taken his eyes and his proud features were melting like wax, streaking into horrible shapes. His skin was yellowing, toasting to burnt orange, plumping up like the flesh was fungus. Mushroom-like growths erupted from the dome of his head, pushed out from his chest.

'Stay away,' Bill gibbered. 'Keep away from me.'

A hideous demon now stood in Morton's place. It was squat, hunched and heavy-set, as tall as a man. Rank, heavy breath hissed from the blotchy slash of its mouth. Bill tried to shout, to warn others – *the beast is only a hell-hound, here is its master.*

But the demon's misshapen claws were already closing round his neck.

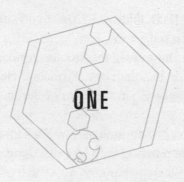

ONE

The stillness of the hillside was torn apart by the grinding of alien engines. Birds clattered from the gorse and heather as a kind of tall, wooden hut burst into bright blue existence. It proclaimed itself to be a police box, but the reality was far stranger and infinitely more exciting.

'Berlin!' cried the Doctor, throwing open the doors. Skinny and dark-eyed, he looked to be in his thirties but was really far older. 'Definitely Berlin.' He took in the woods ahead of him, the damp, scrubby grassland all around and the white-tipped mountains that hemmed in the landscape, and his sharp features hardened further in a frown. 'Sort of. Maybe.' He marched outside, then turned to the slim, attractive black girl who was hovering in the police box's doorway. 'Berlin, d'you think, Martha?'

Martha Jones gave him a look that said, very

eloquently, *Don't think so.* 'How many mountains in Berlin?' she asked.

'Not huge amounts,' the Doctor conceded. 'One or two. In fact… less than one. Probably.' He brightened. 'There's a mountain in the town of Berlin in New York State…'

'I think I've had enough of New York for a while,' said Martha, remembering their last visit there. 'Anyway, we can't be anywhere near a city. Air's too fresh.' There was a playful gleam in her deep brown eyes. 'Is this really 1908, or are we in prehistoric times or something?'

'You suggesting we could be seventy million years off course?' The Doctor tried to give her a look of disapproval, but he couldn't help brightening at the thought. 'That would be *fantastic*, wouldn't it! See any dinosaurs about? I'd say it was unlikely with all the glacial activity that's obviously been shaping the scenery round here, but…' He beamed. 'Look at that valley! That tor! Miss Jones, let's tour the tor.' He grabbed her by the hand and yanked her off on a walk through the heather, his long brown coat flapping round his ankles, his dark suit brightened by a yellow-and-red checked scarf that reminded Martha of Rupert the Bear. Her own outfit was dressier: a gauzy green silk dress with a gold leaf pattern and a close-fitting beaded jacket. But then, she *had* been promised they would be attending a formal function.

'What about this German bloke and his oh-so-important address then?' she asked.

'Old Minkowski! Yeah, if it *is* September 1908, he'll be off to talk to the Assembly of German Naturalists and Physicians, telling them all that space-time is the fourth dimension. Pivotal moment for world physics.' The Doctor laughed. 'Well, he'll just have to bluff his way through without me. We'll stay here dinosaur hunting, just in case. Maybe we could have a prehistoric picnic. Fancy a picnic? I think we should have a picnic…'

Martha smiled and thought back to her old, normal life. Life before she'd picked up with a man who travelled through time and space in a magic police box he called a TARDIS, who whistled past stars and planets like she passed stops on the Circle Line. 'Yeah, well, my family never had too much time for picnics…'

'Well, I really, really like picnics. I like picnic baskets. Especially those ones with the separate little compartments for your knives and forks, that's *genius*—'

The Doctor's enthusiasm was muted by a high-pitched screech of brakes and a loud crashing noise. A cloud of sooty smoke rose up from behind a close-by hillock.

For a moment, Martha and the Doctor shared a wordless look. Then, as one, they ran full pelt towards the sound.

'Car crash?' Martha panted. 'The engine sounded—'

'Throaty, inefficient, and probably downright dangerous…' The Doctor gave her a wild grin. 'I want a go!'

He put on a spurt of speed and reached the brow of the hillock ahead of her. 'Oh, yes!' he cried in delight at what he saw. 'Look at that! An Opel double phaeton.'

'And one slightly crumpled driver,' Martha noted, reaching his side. An old red motor car, quite possibly a close relative of Chitty-Chitty Bang-Bang, had obviously failed to take a sharp corner and was blocking a narrow lane; its bonnet and fenders were bent and scraped after a close encounter with a dry-stone wall. A tall man in a tartan sports coat with a high-standing collar was attempting to push the car away from the wall. A tweed cap was perched on his head of fair curls. He was covered in dirt and grease and had cut his hand quite badly.

'I say!' he called upon sighting the Doctor and Martha. 'Could you offer a chap assistance? Rear wheels locked on the turn. Fiercest sideways skid you ever saw.'

Martha was already making her way down the steep slope to the roadside. The piles of little 'black cherries' dotted around the grass suggested these narrow roads were more used to seeing sheep than motorists. 'What did you do?' she asked, studying his injured hand.

'Sliced it on the blasted fender,' the man said, looking pale. He had a large, beaky nose and brilliant blue eyes. He grinned at her suddenly. 'Excuse the language, my dear. The name's Meredith. Victor Meredith.'

'I'm Martha Jones.' She cast a look at the Doctor, who was lavishing his attention on the car. 'And this is—'

'—an Opel Ten-Eighteen,' said the Doctor, 'pure

elegance from Rüsselsheim.' He caressed the driving seat, which looked more like a cream leather sofa welded to the chassis, and tapped the walnut steering wheel. 'And look! Three-speed epicyclic gearbox with pre-selector control…'

'Indeed yes, and all brand new!' Victor grinned, then winced as Martha whipped his white racing scarf from about his neck. 'You an autocar enthusiast yourself, old buck?'

'Used to be, used to be. I'm the Doctor.'

Victor's eyes turned back to Martha as she wrapped the scarf around his wounded hand. 'And you're his nurse, eh, Miss Jones?'

'Training to be a doctor, actually,' she agreed. *Or I will be in about a century from now.*

'Capital, capital.' Victor smiled. 'Lady doctor, eh? Well, I dare say they do things differently where you're from.'

'Some things.' Martha conceded. 'Are you all right? You're looking a bit wobbly.'

'Can't stand the sight of my own blood,' Victor confessed.

'But animal blood's all right?' The Doctor had pulled a cover from the back seats to reveal a collection of serious-looking shotguns. 'You've got some heavy-duty hunting gear here.'

'That's because I'm here for some heavy-duty hunting,' Victor agreed, flexing his bound hand gingerly. 'The Lakes'll be alive with hunters, I should think.'

'The unspeakable in pursuit of the uneatable…' The Doctor frowned. 'Hang on a minute – Lakes? What, you mean the Lake District?'

'Goodbye, Berlin,' sighed Martha. 'Hello, Pacamac.'

'Lake District, brilliant! I love it round here, the lakes, the waters, the meres… and then there's your tarns, of course, your tiddly little lakes up in the mountains. Tarn…' The Doctor wrapped his lips around the word. 'Good name for a planet, isn't it – Tarn. *Tarrrn*. TARRRRRRR-RRRRRRR-NNNN…'

Victor looked at him bewildered, then turned back to Martha. 'Are you sure you're not his nurse?'

'Miss Jones is an ambassador for the distant land of Freedonia,' the Doctor announced. 'I'm escorting her and seeing she wants for nothing.'

'That'll be the day,' Martha muttered.

'Freedonia – is that one of ours?' wondered Victor. 'Difficult to keep track.'

'Believe me,' Martha told him, 'this is a whole other world for me.'

'Hang about!' boomed the Doctor. 'Lakes alive with hunters?' He reached into the back of the car and hefted a fearsome-looking weapon. 'What's going on? You've got an elephant gun here! Elephants in the Lake District?'

'Bigger game than that.' Victor looked at them both, the colour returning to his cheeks. 'Have you been out of the country just recently?'

Martha grinned at the Doctor. '*Well* out of it.'

'That could explain it then,' said Victor, reaching under the bundle of guns and pulling out a folded newspaper. 'Though I'd have thought the whole world had heard of the Beast of Westmorland…'

Martha took the paper and checked the date. 'September 16th nineteen-oh-*nine*,' she read aloud, with a pointed look at the Doctor.

'Only a year and a few thousand miles out,' he protested. 'Anyway, the car's from Rüsselsheim and *that's* in Germany…'

But then Martha's frown deepened as she saw the headline. 'Beast of Westmorland Found Dead,' she read. 'Battered Prehistoric Killer Washed Up on Lakefront. Experts Baffled.'

'So you can *read* as well as nurse!' said Victor, apparently genuinely impressed.

Martha shot him a look. 'And if I couldn't, there's always this artist's impression.' She frowned at the smear of blotchy ink. 'Looks like… a dinosaur or something.'

'Let me see.' The Doctor snatched the paper from her hands.

'So why all the artillery?' asked Martha. 'Taking this lot along to hunt a dead monster seems a bit like overkill.'

'Friend of mine is the expert naturalist brought in to study the brute – Lord Haleston. He says there's serious injury to its head.' Victor tapped the side of his large nose. 'Thinks perhaps it had a tussle with a mate.'

'Mate?' Martha looked round nervously at the quiet,

beautiful scenery. 'Then there's another thing like that roaming about?'

'There have been one or two sightings,' Victor confirmed. 'Could be just rumours, of course, or hysteria. The police have searched, and the army, too – after the massacre at that village last week they pulled out all the stops. No luck finding anything, but then it's such a wide area to cover…'

'Oh, no. No, no, no.' The Doctor had been studying the paper, stony-faced. Now he slung it in the back of the car. 'Victor, can you give us a lift?'

'The crash has done for the engine, I'm afraid.' Victor sighed. 'Dashed if I can get her to work.'

The Doctor produced his sonic screwdriver, lifted the mangled bonnet and stuck it inside. Then he turned the crank handle and the engine roared into life at once.

Victor stared in baffled delight. 'How'd you do that, then?'

'I want to see this dead monster,' said the Doctor, as if this was explanation enough. 'The paper doesn't say where it is.'

'Naturally. Don't want a circus…'

'Do *you* know?'

'As it happens, yes,' Victor admitted. 'The Beast's pegged out beside the lake at Templewell. We can detour on the way to Goldspur, though I'm not sure I can guarantee you access, old buck. Bit of a closed shop up there, and old Haleston—'

'What's Goldspur?' Martha queried, raising her voice over the engine's sputter.

'Lord Haleston's estate, base of operations for the hunting party,' Victor explained. 'But, wait just a moment! A lady travelling without a trunk? Never thought I'd see the day. Where's your luggage? How'd you pitch up here, in any case?'

'We had a bit of an accident ourselves,' said the Doctor.

'Several,' Martha put in. 'We lost everything and we've been walking all day.'

'Then a lift you shall have,' Victor declared. 'One good turn deserves another, what?' He headed for the driver's seat, but the Doctor was already sat there with an innocent smile.

'I wouldn't dream of making you drive with a bad hand,' the Doctor informed him. 'You ready, then? Come on, stop dawdling!'

Martha allowed Victor to help her climb up beside the Doctor. 'I take it we're joining this monster hunt?' she asked.

The Doctor's fingers drummed on the wheel as Victor clambered into the back. 'I have to be certain what that creature is,' he said ominously.

'I'd *like* to be certain you can drive this thing,' she said. 'How did the sonic screwdriver get it started in two seconds flat?'

The gleam returned to his eyes as he replied. 'My sonic

dealer was giving away a Vintage Earth Engines software bundle free with every Sanctuary Base upgrade.'

As ever, Martha wasn't quite sure if he was talking rubbish or not.

And, as ever, that was all part of the fun.

The Doctor pulled on a lever beside him and stepped on the accelerator pedal, and with a lurch the Opel roared away down the muddy track.

No one noticed the hunched, orange creature hidden in the gorse on the hillside, breathing hoarsely, watching them go with dark, glittering eyes.

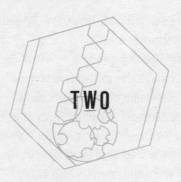

TWO

The car was rattling along at thirty miles an hour, but to Martha it felt more like ninety. She grabbed hold of the underside of the seat while the Doctor whooped and laughed and spun the wheel this way and that, his hair getting windblown into ever less likely styles. The slate-grey sky hung over their heads like an unspoken threat as the car climbed up and down the fells.

'There's a whole gang of us staying with old Haleston,' Victor yelled, trying to stop his fold-out map flapping away like a frightened bird. 'Some have even brought the little ladies along. They're already installed, of course, came on the train.'

'Sensible,' Martha returned, clinging grimly on. 'Why did you decide to drive, then?'

'It's my passion, m'dear! Picked up this little beauty from Manchester, does sixty miles on one oil change.' He stroked the leather upholstery. 'It's not *all* a jaunt, mind. I'm here chiefly on business. Pressing matter to attend to in Kelmore.'

Martha recalled what she'd read of the newspaper article. 'That village the monster attacked?'

'Over forty left dead in the beast's wake, including dear old Sir Albert Morton, it seems. Ran after the monster. Not been seen since.' Victor paused. 'I'm the old boy's lawyer – well, used to be. His papers at the house have been left in a terrible state…'

'So this monster,' said Martha, switching back the subject. 'How come it's strong enough to trash a village but then turns up dead just a few miles away?'

'Perhaps it didn't,' the Doctor pointed out. 'If there have been other sightings since, maybe it's the *living* creature that's the killer.'

'Clearing the name of a dead monster,' Martha observed. 'Sweet.'

'Guilty or innocent, if there *is* a second monster we'll hound it till it cries capivvy,' Victor declared. 'And not just for the sport, or the public service.' He tapped his nose again. 'Those in the know say the King will present a special medal to whoever bags the brute. Er, left here, old buck.'

The Doctor nodded and tackled the crossroads with gusto. Martha spotted a horse and carriage clopping along from the right. A bundle of hunting gear was tied to the roof of the carriage.

'Looks like you've got competition,' Martha observed.

'Let them come.' Victor folded the map and leaned back in his seat. 'The more the merrier.' The car slowed, the engine growling in protest as the Doctor turned onto a steep hillside track. 'Ah, Templewell!' said Victor brightly. 'Here be monsters. Dead ones, at any rate.'

As they turned the next corner, the Doctor slowed the car further. A policeman on a black, shiny bicycle was blocking a dirt track leading off from the roadside. His uniform was smart, with brass buttons dazzling to the eye. He wore a moustache like a clothes brush beneath his red nose.

'You'll have to back up,' said the policeman in a thick northern accent. 'This road is closed.'

'Good, I'm glad. Can't be too careful,' the Doctor informed him. 'Don't want just anyone getting down there to see the monster, eh? We're with Lord Haleston.'

Victor stood up in the back. 'Tell him Victor Meredith's arrived with, er, experts from London.'

The policeman looked doubtfully at Martha. 'Experts, is it?'

'Tell you what,' said the Doctor, jumping from the car, his coattails flapping. 'We'll tell him ourselves.' He pushed past the policeman. 'This way?'

'You can't go down there!' the policeman protested.

'And you can't come after us,' Martha informed him, putting on her most genteel tones as she hurried after the Doctor. 'I mean, wouldn't do to leave the road unguarded, would it?'

The policeman was left gaping as Victor gave him a cheery wave and followed them down the footpath.

'Good work,' said Victor, chuckling to himself. 'I knew from the first we would all get along! Ah, Doctor, it's just a pity you're not a hunting man…'

The Doctor's hands were shoved deep in his pockets as he strode along. 'Oh, I never said that.'

They moved quickly down the quiet track. Sheep and cattle watched them languidly from adjacent fields, the only observers. Then, as the path wound round the hillside, Martha caught a glimpse of grey water and a huge, dark shape beyond the high hedgerows. She parted some wet leafy branches and peered through, and the Doctor pressed his face up beside her to see.

'Oh my god…' Martha felt sick just taking in the sheer size of the beast lying on the shore far below. Only the upper body was protruding from the muddy swell of the lake, but that alone was as long as a playing field. Men were milling around it, dwarfed by its mass. The creature's corpse lay on its side, two huge clawed paws clasped together in some sick parody of prayer. Its neck was as long and thick as a battleship, leading to a set of hideous jaws, each twice as long as a train carriage and crammed with ivory spikes. But above the jaws was little more than a mangled mess of blackened bone. Most of the head seemed to have been ripped clear away.

'What d'you think it died of?' Martha deadpanned.

The Doctor puffed out a long breath. 'I didn't think

anything could kill a Skarasen.'

'A what?'

'A cyborg animal – part organic, part metal. Part reared, part engineered.'

Martha shivered. 'You've met one before?'

'A little one,' the Doctor confessed. 'You could say I got under its feet. But that was ages ago, up in Loch Ness and about seventy years from now.'

'Loch Ness?' Martha stared at him, incredulous. 'You mean there really is a monster—?'

'Onwards we trot!' called Victor, who was waiting for them further down the track. 'I feel a view up close is in order, don't you?'

The Doctor was about to follow, when Martha held him back. 'If this Skarasen is a cyborg… then who made it?'

'Zygons,' said the Doctor, his dark eyes troubled.

'And you've come up against Zygons too?'

'Oh, yes. And the ones I met never said anything about having *two* Skarasens, so…' Abruptly, he hurried away after Victor. 'This doesn't feel right. We need to find out exactly what's going on round here, and pronto. *Prontissimo.* Pronto-a-go-go.' He turned and gave her a wide grin. 'Come on, then, you heard the man. Onwards we trot…'

Steeling herself, Martha jogged down with him to face up to the mauled monster.

* * *

Lord Henry Haleston was not enjoying his day. His assistants and orderlies were giving him a wide berth, and he didn't blame them. How the Prime Minister expected him to compile a serious-minded report on *this*...

There were two great passions in Lord Haleston's life – one was amassing facts about the natural world, the other was placing those facts in a proper, sensible order. He had spent most of his fifty-seven years doing exactly that, patiently and meticulously ordering the great pattern of living things.

Now here he was, faced with something on his very doorstep that not only upset the applecart but also dashed it into a thousand pieces.

And as the young man in the strange suit and overcoat came bounding towards him, a striking girl from the colonies close on his heels, he sensed at once that here was something else come to stamp upon those cart-splinters. But at least it was something he could shout at.

'Who the devil are you two?' Haleston demanded. 'This area is closed to press and public alike. What do you mean by barging into a secret government enquiry?'

But the young man spoke at a pace and foghorn volume that matched his own exactly. 'I'm the Doctor and this is Miss Martha Jones, your grace. I'm an expert in, oohhh, most things, really; she's an expert in the very latest medical training. And when you've listened to what I've got to say you'll probably need some!' He drew a deep breath and smiled cockily at the stunned onlookers. 'And as if all *that* wasn't enough, Mr Victor Meredith will now vouch for us. Here he is!'

Haleston blinked as Victor's concerned face poked out from behind one of the beast's colossal claws. 'I'll vouch for the Doctor, all right, Henry. And the young lady's a visitor from Freedonia, you know. Pin sharp and bright as a button.'

'Really, Victor.' Haleston frowned. 'I'm afraid I'm most fearfully busy, so if you've satisfied your curiosity and that of your friends…?'

'Satisfied, Henry? I should say *not!*' Victor stared at one of the creature's weighty talons. 'You never said the brute was this enormous or I'd have brought a dozen cannon instead of the four-bore!'

'Oh, by the way, H.H. sends his regards, Lord Haleston,' the Doctor announced suddenly, 'and hopes your enquiry will soon be concluded successfully.'

'H.H.?' Haleston blinked. 'Do you mean to tell me, sir, that you are an emissary of our Prime Minister, Mr Asquith?'

'Emissary? He's a mate of mine!' The Doctor bounded over to study the fallen monster's fearful teeth. 'We've had some wild times, me and H.H., let me tell you. I remember this one time there was me, H.H., Dave "The Rave" Lloyd George and this leaky bottle of soda water, right…'

'The Doctor has certain specialist knowledge he believes may help with your enquiry,' Martha broke in, with a warm smile. 'In the interests of public safety he thought it a good idea to share it.'

'Oh?' Haleston's eyes narrowed. 'A dependable sighting of this other beast rumoured to be on the loose?'

'Not quite,' she told him. 'But important anyway.'

'Hmm. Seems you're *another* piece of the puzzle that doesn't fit,' said Haleston more gently. 'An erudite and gentle maiden accompanying such a cocksure young rip!'

'Cocksure, that's me,' the Doctor agreed, circling the giant, devastated head of the beast. 'Cocksure that this creature and the other beast that's been sighted are not of Earthly origin.'

Haleston stared. 'Not of Earthly origin?'

'Oh, come on, your lordship, that's not such a big leap of imagination for a man of learning like yourself, surely?' He grabbed a hacksaw from one of the orderlies. 'You haven't been able to shave off a single scrap of skin, have you? You've sawed and chopped and hacked away, but you haven't made a mark, right? Am I right? I'm right.' He banged the saw against a shard of the creature's skull. The bone chimed like a bell.

'Metal,' said Martha quietly as the chime died away.

'An alloy not known on this planet,' the Doctor agreed, now peering to inspect two of the enormous teeth. 'And tell me, Lord Haleston, in your considerable experience, have you ever come across a living creature with a cranium constructed of so dense a material as—?' He broke off, scrubbed at something close to the monster's gum line. 'Whoops, you're a politician, aren't you? You spend your life surrounded by them.'

'Kindly keep your hands off the specimen!' Haleston bristled. 'And, may I add, this is not a matter for levity, sir!'

'Very true!' The Doctor snatched his hand from out between the monster's teeth and stuffed it in his pocket. 'Good point, excellent, I'm glad you brought that up.' He squared up to Lord Haleston. 'Frankly, I'd say it was a matter for panic, pandemonium and searching questions in very high places. Because here's the newsflash: we have in front of us a giant aquatic cyborg that can't be stopped by anything on Earth – and yet it's been stopped. Seriously, top-of-the-head-blown-apart sort of stopped.'

Martha nodded. 'But stopped by what?'

The Doctor gestured to the beast's shattered cranium. 'The damage here suggests an intense heat and a very sudden impact – from *within* the head.'

'I had come to the same conclusion,' said Haleston, grudgingly.

Victor's mouth had been flapping open and shut but now he finally forced out in an incredulous tone: 'But… whatever could cause such a thing?'

'My best guess is some kind of hunter from an alien planet with weapons of unspeakable power, which if deployed without care could cause far more damage and loss of life than your Beast of Westmorland ever could.' The Doctor suddenly grinned, looked round at his astounded audience and rubbed his hands together. 'Right, then! Who feels they could use some of that medical attention I mentioned, hmm?'

THREE

'Well, going for the subtle approach really worked, didn't it?' Martha looked at the Doctor as he drove them through the darkening evening. 'Ooh! Hang on, what's this?' She put a finger to his ear and pretended to stare at it closely. 'Oh yes, it's the flea in your ear Haleston sent you away with, for asking him to believe in two lots of aliens on the same day.'

The Doctor shrugged as he slowed down at a crossroads. 'Is it my fault you humans have got such closed minds? I only hope this alien hunter doesn't blow them wide open.'

Martha frowned. 'Why would an alien hunter bother with humans if it's after this other Skarasen?'

'D'you reckon Victor would cry much if a stray rabbit caught the shot he'd meant for a grouse?'

'Um... possibly not.' She looked back at Victor, who was snoring quite calmly in the back, a noise that rivalled the chugging engine for volume. 'Taking it all very calmly, isn't he?'

'Stoic's the word,' the Doctor agreed, as they rattled away down yet another country lane.

Victor had, it seemed, been prepared to countenance a metallic dinosaur staring him in the face. But, at the thought of 'big game hunters from Mars', he'd simply guffawed, clapped the Doctor heartily on the back and led him quickly back to the car before Haleston's oaths could grow any more colourful. After all, there was a lady present.

Martha shivered, grateful for the Doctor's coat about her shoulders. Her outfit offered little protection from the chill wind, and the dark clouds billowing overhead promised rain. They were just as grey and formless as the landscape stretching out around them, softened with the fall of dusk.

'So, while there's no one to heckle,' said Martha, 'tell me more about the Zygons.'

'A bunch of them crash-landed in Scotland centuries ago,' the Doctor recalled. 'They thought they were alone on the planet, sat there underneath Loch Ness with their little pet, quietly plotting to take over the world. Didn't mention popping down to the Lakes now and then to borrow a pint of Skarasen milk.'

'Milk?' She looked at him. 'That's a joke, yeah?'

He shook his head. 'The Zygons depend on a Skarasen's lactic fluid for food. Without it they'd die.'

Martha shuddered. 'You'd want to make sure your hands were warm before trying to milk *that* thing.'

'And bring one hell of a bucket,' the Doctor agreed.

Suddenly there was a blur of motion ahead of them. Martha shrieked as a dark shape rolled down from the steep hillside in front of the car, blocking their way, and the Doctor stamped on the brakes. The rear wheels locked and whistled, and, for a terrifying moment, Martha thought she was going to go flying through the windscreen. She managed to hold on, but a thumping impact in the back of the seat told her that the sleeping Victor hadn't fared so well.

The car screeched to a halt centimetres from the object in the road, and the Doctor quickly turned to check on Victor, sprawled in the foot well with his rifles. 'He's out cold, bumped his head. But I think—'

An awful keening, gurgling noise, somewhere between a blocked drain and a cry for help, rose up from the road ahead of them.

The Doctor jumped out of the car, and Martha quickly followed him. With a tightening of her guts, she saw what had fallen to block their way. It was panting wildly for breath, rocking on its back like a baby.

And it was alien.

The thing was orange-red with a huge, domed forehead, covered in thick, mushroom-like growths. Its features were all bunched up in the middle of its face, and it had no neck or shoulders – the head seemed to sprout straight from the torso, which looked like giant spots had burst all over it. Thick, crusty nodules ran down the creature's chest like horrible buttons.

The Doctor started feeling about the grotesque body as if looking for a pulse. 'Speak of the Zygons, and one'll come rolling down a hillside at you.'

'*This* is a Zygon?' Martha breathed. She saw now that there was a gaping, sticky wound at the back of the oversized head, and its legs were a butchered mess, crusted in thick, dark blood. She caught a feral look in the alien's eyes. They were the eyes not simply of a creature in pain – but of a creature that hated.

Then, with a mournful, sink-emptying sound, its chest fell still.

'Dead?' she ventured quietly.

The Doctor nodded. 'Afraid so. If we'd got him talking, perhaps he could have told us something about— No!' He shouted down at the body: 'Oh, come on, don't do that!'

'Do what?' Martha stared at him – then became aware of a high-pitched whine in the air. She looked back at the Zygon's body in time to see it glow with light and fade away to nothingness. 'Is that normal?' she whispered.

Frustrated, the Doctor slapped his hand down on the track where the Zygon had been. 'Molecular dispersal,' he said. 'The life signs of the crew are monitored from their ship's control room. If one of them dies, the body can be zapped into particles like it was never here…'

Martha looked around warily in case any others might be about to follow it. 'How d'you think it got those injuries? It didn't pick them up in the fall.'

'True. So whatever did for him could still be about up there. Let's take a look!' With that he went dashing off up the scree-covered hillside, his suit jacket flapping about him in the gusting wind.

Sighing to herself, Martha ran after him – glad she'd decided to wear flat shoes today, but terrified of what she might find waiting at the top of the rise. It was more exposed up here. A few cows were grazing, unbothered by the vicious squalls of peppering rain.

'This is no good.' The Doctor squinted into the grey, spongy landscape of shadows. 'Can't see a thing. Whatever took a pop at that Zygon, it could be anywhere now.' He looked at the cows. 'Sorry to bother you, ladies, but have you seen anything big and nasty pass this way?'

Unsurprisingly, the cows ignored him. Martha shivered. She suddenly realised just how dark it was. No twinkling city lights in the distance, no street lamps. Just her and the Doctor, and the cold, blustery night.

'This alien hunter you were on about,' she said, pulling the overcoat closer around her. 'Looks like it's after the Zygons as well as their Skarasens.'

'I wonder who they've upset,' the Doctor mused. 'I also wonder how many Zygons there are around here – and what they're planning to do about it…'

'Doctor!'

Both Martha and the Doctor started at the frantic shout. It was Victor. Straight away, the Doctor was off and running down the hillside, barely keeping his balance as his plimsolls slipped and skidded on the wet grass. Martha wasn't so lucky, sliding a good deal of the way down on her bum.

Victor was sitting up in the back of the car, pointing down the winding lane, towards a shadowy hillside. 'Over there. Came out of nowhere…'

Martha followed the arrow of his finger – and, as scudding clouds fled the half-moon's spotlight, she felt a chill go through her.

There was a figure on the hillside. The figure of a young girl, maybe eight or nine, with pale skin and long blonde hair. As if mimicking Victor, she raised her arm, pointing away from them into the furrowed ridges of the distant darkness.

Then the moonlight dimmed as fresh clouds clustered. When they had passed on, the girl had gone too.

The Doctor turned to Martha, eyes wide and bright. 'Did you see that?'

She nodded uneasily. 'A girl. Pointing.'

'A phantom,' whispered Victor, dabbing at the bump on his head. 'With an unearthly message from the other side!'

'The other side of the valley, maybe,' said Martha. 'What's over there?'

'Toombs' Fell, Wolvenlath Mere…' Victor shrugged. 'Difficult terrain, not for your tourists.'

'This is *the* night for spotting things!' the Doctor enthused. 'One giant water-monster, one phantom child, one shape-shifting alien, a couple of cows…'

'Er, excuse me?' Martha grabbed his arm. '*Shape-shifting* alien?'

'Did I not mention that?' He gave his wide-eyed innocent look. 'Zygons have body-print technology. They capture people and keep them on board their ship – while they go out and take their victims' places in the human world.'

Martha looked at him in dismay. 'That's not good. Because if these Zygons *are* being hunted, what better place to hide than in someone else's body?'

'Whatever are you talking about?' Victor demanded. 'Why have we stopped, anyway? What happened to my head?' By now he was looking mildly affronted. 'What are we even doing here?'

'Lots of questions,' mused the Doctor, jumping back into the driver's seat. 'Y'know, I think it's time we got you home, big fella. *Then* I think it's time that Martha and I went on a little hunt of our own.'

'Oh?' Martha wasn't sure she liked the sound of that. 'Hunting what, exactly?'

The Doctor grinned and stamped on the accelerator. 'Answers!' he yelled, and, with a grind of sticking gears, the Opel roared away.

FOUR

Edward Lunn crept through the dark, wet forest, a four-bore shotgun clamped tightly in both hands. Teazel went ahead of him, his bristly tail wagging. Every few seconds, the fawn English Mastiff would stop to sniff at piles of mulchy leaves or a fallen tree; no doubt about it, he had got the scent of something.

Lunn barely felt the coldness of the encroaching night, and he certainly felt no fear. So much of his life was spent hemmed in by the dreary mahogany of his offices… This was his release! The moonlight was fitful but strong enough to see by. He had his gun and his dog, and he was not about to give up this most promising trail for polite company and a game of cards back at Goldspur.

'Good lad, Teazel,' he whispered. 'Who's going to lead Daddy to the big kill then, eh?'

He'd passed a number of broken trees now, the trunks crushed to splinters. It boded well, as he knew neither police nor soldiers had yet scoured the land around Wolvenlath. And while there were many hunters at large in the District, Lunn had seen none take the same trails as he. He could be in with a real chance of sniffing out the lair of this beast, and that could mean a medal when the King paid his visit…

Suddenly, Teazel stopped dead before a tangled thicket. His tail held still. He had seen something.

'Here we go, then,' Lunn muttered to himself, a thrill going through him as he held up his gun in readiness. He peered through the twisted branches and saw something moving in a small clearing beyond. He couldn't see much detail in the moonlight but enough to be sure this was no great beast. It was the size and shape of a man, hunched over, peering about for something. Lunn felt a flash of disappointment. So much for being the only hunter on this patch…

But then the figure turned sideways on, and a gasp escaped Lunn's lips. This was no man. It was some inhuman monster. Its huge head sprouted straight from its chest, lending it a disturbing, almost foetal appearance.

Obliging of you to give me such a big, fat target, thought Lunn, bringing the shotgun up shakily to his shoulder. 'Time you went back to hell, whatever you are…'

Then he heard the wet crack of a stick, snapping close behind him. Teazel started barking. Lunn whirled around to find another of the creatures was creeping up behind him. Its eyes blazed with malice as it reached out with twisted fingers and lunged for his throat.

Horrified, Lunn opened fire. The shot went wide, but Teazel threw himself at the monster, barking furiously, his teeth tearing at its orange flesh, driving it back.

Lunn turned to find the first monster was now running towards him. He crashed away through the wet wood and bracken, the rasp of his breath loud in his ears. But not loud enough to drown out the howl of his dog in the thick of the forest behind him.

He ran on and on, forcing his way through bushes and brambles, until suddenly he found himself out in the open. The dark sky was furry with cloud, the sleepy eye of the half-moon gazing down on the shadow-world below. He heard more crashes behind him. The things were still coming after him. He had to reload his shotgun—

But there was another one here in the field. He caught a glimpse of its dark form as it ducked under a fence and came running towards him.

Cursing under his breath, his heart pounding wildly, Lunn staggered off again through the thick mud of the fresh-ploughed field. It led onto a slope of pasture. At least it was a downhill run, he was grateful for that.

Until he saw that at the end of the slope there was nowhere to go. He had reached the edge of the fell, with only a steep, sheer drop down to the waters of Wolvenlath Mere.

They're herding me towards it, he realised.

Lunn stumbled to a halt close to the straggly hedges that guarded the lip of the precipice. Then he turned to face the sinister beasts. There were five of them now: one cutting off his flight to the left, one guarding the path to the right, three more closing on him from the front. Mechanically, he reloaded the shotgun. But he knew that even if he downed one of these devils, the others would get him. And then...

'Human,' rasped one of the creatures in a gurgling whisper.

The beasts can speak.

'Stay back,' he called in a high, wavering voice, willing his fingers to work, his hands to stop shaking. 'Stay away from me!'

'Remain still.' The night-creatures were closing on him. 'You cannot escape.'

'We have need of you,' hissed another.

Lunn stared round at the beasts. 'Can't escape, you say?' He blasted at the nearest of the creatures. Its death cry rent the air as he turned and blundered through the hedges at the cliff edge, holding his breath.

'Pursue!' came the terrible, inhuman hiss as they ran to get him.

Lunn shut his eyes, and not a whimper escaped his lips as the ground fell away beneath his feet.

'Here we are then,' announced the Doctor, rolling up in

the car beside an ornate stone archway crowned with intricately carved ivy. 'Excess marks the spot.'

Martha saw a brass plaque declaring that this was the Goldspur estate. 'And not before time,' she said, rubbing the small of her bruised back. The last mile had been especially bumpy, the narrow muddy lanes churned up and potholed.

'Splendid run, chauffeur,' called Victor. 'Got a place to stay? Or are you dossing in the pure, tonight?'

The Doctor considered. 'Maybe if we sweet-talked old Haleston…'

Martha shook her head. 'No way. They'd take one look and stick me downstairs with the servants.' She frowned. 'And even if they didn't, I've seen *Gosford Park*! You need two changes of outfit just to go to the loo. Me – one dress. One crumpled, dirty, dishevelled dress. So we are not going in there tonight. OK?'

The Doctor reflected on this outburst for a moment, then turned to Victor. 'Any good hotels in the area? B and Bs? Tents?' He glanced back at Martha. 'How do we feel about tents?'

'No tents.'

'No tents… Gypsy caravan? Stable? There's this police box I know of, but…'

'There's quite a decent hunting lodge that borders the back of the estate,' said Victor cheerfully. 'About a half-mile round the track. Popular with tourists come high season, but at this time of year, they may have room.' He flexed his bandaged hand. 'I think the war wound's up to it – hop back in and I'll take you.'

Martha considered walking. Then she thought of the eerie apparition of the small girl out in the wilderness. She consulted with her spine and decided that perhaps they were both feeling up to one last jaunt in the motor car after all.

An hour later, Martha was feeling happier. Mrs Unswick, the owner of the Lodge, was a plump woman in her fifties with long, plaited hair and a knowing look in her eyes. At first, she had seemed suspicious of her prospective guests' lack of luggage. But Victor had vouched for them, the Doctor had chatted the old girl up a bit, and soon she was happily revealing she only had one other paying guest that night and would be glad to make a couple of rooms available.

Martha had bagsied the one with the biggest bed and, after a ruthless tournament of stone-scissors-paper, had also won the right to the first bath. Only when she realised it was a tin bath and a jug of hot water in a freezing cold room did she wonder if the Doctor had played to lose.

After a quick clean up which left her shivering even under five blankets, Martha discovered fresh clothes in the wardrobe – a long fawn overcoat, a flowing khaki wool skirt trimmed with black satin and a woollen shirt-blouse patterned with a dark check. With delight, she wriggled into the warm checks, pulled on the skirt and went downstairs.

She found the Doctor in the sitting room with Mrs Unswick, in front of the fire. It was a large room that seemed smaller thanks to the heavy drapes, densely striped wallpaper and so many dark wooden cabinets dotted about, crammed with china ornaments. A stag's head stared glassily out from a plaque on the wall, with framed maps of the area on either side.

'Ah! Clara's clothes suit you very well,' said Mrs Unswick approvingly.

'Thank you for the loan – I can give the Doctor his coat back now.' Martha smiled. 'Is Clara your daughter?'

'Goodness no, my chickabiddy!' The large woman gave a laugh that rattled the china. 'Never had time for kiddies, not in my London days and certainly not now. Clara worked here as my maid till a week ago. I had to let her go – always sticking her beak into other people's business, was Clara.'

The Doctor raised his eyebrows. 'And so you took her clothes?'

'Compensation!' said Mrs Unswick firmly. 'She made off in the night with some of my best silver! Still, it's all done with now. Like... poor little Molly Melton.'

'Mrs U thinks we saw a ghost this evening,' said the Doctor, his eyes agleam.

'The poor girl went missing from the fields round Kelmore two weeks ago,' Mrs Unswick explained.

'Molly was always one to play a little too far from home, they say. And one night she never came back. A week after that, the village lay in ruins. Some say they saw Molly just standing there, watching it all. Like a vengeful wraith, making certain no one else would ever come home in her place. And now it's said she points the way to danger... Warning the innocent away.'

'Never thought of myself as innocent before,' said Martha.

But Mrs U had finished her tale, and the only sound was the crack and spit of logs in the fire and the heavy tick of the clock on the mantel, the only movement the dance of the woman's shadow in the firelight.

'Of course, Molly *could* have been abducted by shape-changing creatures from another world,' the Doctor suggested brightly.

'Don't be ridiculous, Doctor,' Mrs Unswick chided. 'She's a spirit, and that's that.'

'A sprightly spirit. She had it away on her ghostly toes in a blink...' The Doctor got up and looked at the framed map. 'Ah! The surrounding area. Now, we left Lord Haleston and his little discovery here...' He started tracing his finger along a pathway. 'We stopped the car when our friend fell into the road here, and Molly's image appeared to us... here!' He tapped the glass. 'Yep, pointing towards Wolvenlath, just as Victor said.' He looked enquiringly at Mrs Unswick. 'Any dangers to the innocent there that you know about?'

The woman shrugged. 'The walking's difficult, so the tourists stay clear. Few souls about at any time.'

Martha's eyes met the Doctor's. 'Good place for something to hide?'

Just then there was a crash from the doorway behind them. Martha and the Doctor turned in surprise to find an athletic-looking man in loud-checked trousers, a dark waistcoat and rolled-up shirtsleeves, struggling into the room with a large, battered leather box. Lenses and eyepieces protruded from the thing in his arms as well as various brass levers and handles.

'May I trouble you for more of your late husband's insulation tape, Mrs Unswick?' he asked in slightly accented English. Then he noticed the Doctor and Martha. 'Oh, please forgive my intrusion.'

'No intrusion,' the Doctor assured him.

Mrs Unswick rose from her chair with some difficulty. 'I'll just fetch your tape, Monsieur, and let you introduce yourselves.' So saying, she bustled from the room.

The Frenchman gave a small bow, and smiled at the Doctor and Martha – particularly at Martha. 'Claude Romand, at your service.'

'I'm the Doctor, this is Martha Jones, and this is a Pathé film camera you're carrying, isn't it!' He grinned. 'Can I see?'

'You work for the newsreels yourself?' Romand looked suddenly guarded. 'I hope you are not here to – how do the Americans put it – scoop me?'

'I'm an explorer,' the Doctor informed him, 'among other things.' He took the large box from Romand, staring at it like a boy with a new toy.

'You're a journalist, Mr Romand?' asked Martha.

'I have been dispatched by News of the Globe in Paris to report on the strange events unfolding here,' he agreed. 'Alas, my camera's refusal to focus is proving stranger than all else.'

'Well, a precision instrument like this, it's bound to go out of alignment from time to time…' The Doctor placed the camera down on the floor with due reverence – and then whacked the back of it with his fist. 'Try it now.'

Romand stooped to pick up the camera, peered through the eyepiece attached to the side, and moved a sliding lever. 'You have a magic touch, my dear sir!' He grinned, set down the camera and embraced the Doctor. Then he turned to Martha hopefully.

She raised her eyebrows at him, and folded her arms.

Sheepishly, Romand turned back to the Doctor. 'So, Doctor. You are an explorer, yes? Then you have come here because of the Beast of Westmorland, as I have?'

'Pretty much,' the Doctor agreed. 'Any sightings yet? Captured anything on film?'

'No sightings,' said Romand, more subdued now. 'But I have visited Kelmore. The destruction there is…' He broke off, as if groping for the right English words to describe it. But the words did not come. 'My editor thought these stories a big joke, he sent me here for a light-hearted piece. He does not understand… this thing must be found, and captured, and *destroyed*.' Abruptly his mood lightened as he turned again to Martha. 'But forgive me, speaking of such things before a lady…'

'Oh, shut up,' Martha told him good-naturedly. 'What damage was done? What have you seen?'

Romand hesitated. 'As it happens, I have had some stock developed at the request of the police. Manpower is limited, and they hope that screening my films in public places will provide them with volunteers, yes? And these reels, they are not collected until tomorrow…'

The Doctor brightened. 'So, you have the reels – do you have a projector?'

'In my room, dear sir.'

Martha smiled. 'Then how about we go there right now and you can show us your footage?'

'Bet you don't get an offer like that everyday, eh, Monsieur?' The Doctor grinned. 'Not even in Paris!'

Mrs Unswick shuffled back into the sitting room with a small black reel. Martha thought the woman looked somehow older now in the firelight. 'Here's your tape, Monsieur.'

'We're after bigger reels than that, Mrs U!' cried the Doctor, dropping briefly into an American accent. 'It's show time! Movie screening upstairs, in Monsieur Romand's room. The original home cinema! Do we have any choc-ices? I like choc-ices, the proper ones you get from ice-cream vans. No? Never mind…' He ushered Romand and Martha through the door. 'We've got lights, we've got camera – all we need now is action!'

FIVE

Martha slept uneasily that night. The flickering, jerky black-and-white images she'd seen on Romand's projector screen haunted her thoughts. CNN it wasn't. Disturbing it was, and big-time.

It was so weird, looking at images that seemed so ancient and yet knowing they had only happened a couple of days ago. The grief, the confusion she'd seen would still be etched on the villagers' faces. The smashed-in houses, the trampled gardens, the ruined church – and, more likely than not, those monster footprints – would all be visible too.

She checked her watch by the light of the candle on the bedside table. It was after three in the morning, and still she felt wide awake. That was the problem with TARDIS travel, you never really knew what time it was or when you should be sleeping. Was it jet lag, or *time* lag, or—

A sudden banging on the door made her sit bolt upright. She threw on Clara's clothes and got up.

'Whatever's the commotion?' Mrs Unswick's weary voice floated up from the hallway downstairs. 'Who's there?'

'Victor Meredith,' came the familiar voice. 'I'm afraid it's an emergency, Mrs Unswick. I'm calling for Miss Jones… or the Doctor…'

Martha burst out onto the landing – only to find the Doctor was already running down the stairs in his suit, his coat under one arm, cupping the stub of a candle to light his way. She hurried after him.

Mrs Unswick was also still dressed. She opened the door, and Victor stepped inside. He looked pale and flustered in the candlelight, his overcoat thrown on over blue flannel pyjamas.

'What's happened?' the Doctor demanded.

'Apologies and all that,' said Victor. 'It's a friend of mine, Eddie Lunn – part of the hunting party – he went missing this evening. We were all worried sick, of course, only now he's turned up in a bad way. Crack on the head, can't get any sense out of him…' He looked at Martha and held up his bad hand, now sporting a sticking plaster. 'Haleston can't rouse his own doctor, and given the miracles you worked on my little scratch this afternoon I wondered if you might consider…?'

'We'd better get going,' said Martha, leading the way out through the door into the cold night. The Opel's engine had been left running. She got into the back seat and the Doctor slid in beside her. Then, with a wave to the bewildered Mrs Unswick, they set off at a fast roar for Goldspur.

Soon they were driving through the moonlit gardens and topiaries up to the house. Viewed from the front, it was a huge, forbidding rectangle of stone and ivy. A butler was waiting attentively by the front door. He almost went cross-eyed at the sight of Martha, who simply glared at him as she followed Victor and the Doctor inside.

The entrance hall was just as opulent and draughty as she'd expected, and the fancy spiral staircase that twisted up to the landing was like something off a movie set. The butler, Chivvers, led the three of them into a bedroom lit smokily by oil lamps.

A pale, handsome man lay in the middle of a four-poster with a crooked bandage round his head. There were deep scratches down his face and neck. On one side of him sat a petite woman with ivory skin and blonde hair arranged in a bun, holding his hand. Lord Haleston, dressed formally in a lounge suit, stood by the window, eyeing the Doctor suspiciously.

'It's good of you to come at this hour, since my own man's indisposed,' he said slowly. 'But we'll have none of your crank scaremongering here, please, Doctor.'

Martha gave him a look. 'I'll be examining the patient,'

she said. 'Mrs Lunn? Have you cleaned these cuts and abrasions?'

The woman nodded, looking slightly dazed. 'It hurt him, so I stopped. I… I fear that his mind still suffers.'

'How is his head?' She pulled at the crooked bandage round Lunn's forehead. It fell away to reveal a nasty, purpling swell with a crusted bloody gash in its centre.

'Told you,' said Victor. 'It's a real sockdologer.'

The Doctor slipped on his chunky glasses and took a closer look at Lunn. 'I'd say he's fallen some distance, wouldn't you, Miss Jones?'

She opened the top button of Lunn's pyjamas to expose more angry welts. 'Slid some of the way too, looking at these scrapes.'

'I knew something was wrong when Teazel came home without him,' said Mrs Lunn, still out of it, her voice barely more than a whisper. 'Teazel is Eddie's dog, do you see? He never leaves his side. And yet, the wound on the poor animal's back…'

'What kind of wound?' Martha asked.

'I've never seen a marking like it,' mumbled Haleston.

'Eddie came back not half an hour ago,' Victor went on, 'clinging to the back of his horse, black and blue, soaking wet, in a terrible state.'

Just then Martha caught a bob of movement from the doorway. She saw a boy with neatly combed red hair peeping round furtively. Clearly he wasn't supposed to be up.

He looked at Martha and mouthed: 'Is my father all right?'

'He will be,' she mouthed back discreetly.

Looking a little happier, the boy disappeared once more from sight.

Martha started to feel for Mr Lunn's pulse. Abruptly, he stirred, moaning like a man waking from a bad dream. Then his eyes snapped open; they were a staring, piercing blue. He looked up at Martha and his face twisted into a scowl. 'Get off me. Keep away from me.'

Martha held up her hands and duly backed away. 'So much for polite society.'

'Do you remember what happened, Edward?' said Haleston, crossing to join them around the bed.

Lunn's face twisted, his breathing became hoarser. 'Wolvenlath…' he said. 'Hunting… in Wolvenlath…'

'Is that where you were tonight, Edward?' Haleston demanded.

'The little girl on the hillside,' Victor remembered. 'She was pointing the way to Wolvenlath.'

Mrs Lunn looked at him anxiously. 'An omen?'

'I saw her,' Lunn whispered. 'Pointing…'

'What else did you see in Wolvenlath, Eddie?' the Doctor urged him.

'Can't remember…' Lunn put his hand to his head. 'We must go there… Find… what attacked me. Something… in the forest… in the *water*…'

'Poor soul's delusional,' said Haleston bluntly.

'He's survived a deeply traumatic experience,' said the Doctor, a sharp edge to his voice. 'That can turn anyone a little crazy for a time, believe me.'

'It's possible the crack to his head has given him concussion,' said Martha, in a more reasonable tone. 'That can cause memory loss, disorientation…' She looked at the Doctor and lowered her voice. 'Are there X-ray machines yet?'

He nodded genially. 'Getting there.'

'No X-rays,' Lunn snapped suddenly.

Martha gave him a funny look. 'But you may have a fractured skull, in which case—'

'No X-rays,' he repeated.

Mrs Lunn looked baffled. 'X-rays…?'

'I'll not submit to that hocus-pocus,' said Lunn. 'D'you hear?'

The Doctor shrugged at Martha. 'As a medical aid, X-rays are in their infancy right now,' he said quietly. 'Shock of the new, and all that…'

'All right.' Martha sighed. 'Well, Mr Lunn, you should stay in bed under observation for the next two or three days—'

'Watching me,' Lunn muttered. '*Wanting* me…' He stared round wildly. 'We have to go there, Henry. Hunt this thing. Have to find…'

'Yes?' The Doctor leaned forwards. 'What do we have to find?'

'Patient's getting agitated, Doctor…' Martha placed

her hands on Lunn's shoulders and eased him back down into a lying position. 'Try to rest, now.'

As she spoke, a massive, muscular Mastiff trotted in, its short tail wagging, and sat by his master's side. Lunn saw his dog and at once he calmed, reached out a hand to pat its head, started to breathe more deeply.

'That's better,' Martha murmured.

'The trusty Teazel, I presume.' The Doctor reached down to fuss the Mastiff's dark ears – and then frowned at the huge welt that had risen on the dog's back. The skin had blackened the fawn-coloured fur around it, and the wound was starting to fester. 'Looks like… a sting of some kind.'

Haleston harrumphed. 'I'd like to know what on Earth could sting like that.'

The Doctor looked at him. 'You wouldn't.'

Martha turned quickly to Victor. 'We'll need some more warm water and a soft cloth to finish cleaning up those abrasions, and the dog's wound too.'

Victor looked out of his depth almost at once. 'You're asking me?'

'Tell Chivvers,' said Haleston, 'he'll fetch them.'

Suddenly, Teazel started barking and sniffing at the Doctor's coat pocket.

Martha frowned. 'Got a Scooby snack in there?'

The Doctor patted his pocket and frowned. 'P'raps we should be off.' He jumped up from the bed and headed to the door with Victor. 'It's late, we're tired…'

'And tomorrow, the hunt is on,' said Haleston.

The Doctor paused. 'You're going to Wolvenlath?'

'Naturally, we are,' said Victor. 'You can see the state Eddie's in. This thing is a menace. It has to be stopped.'

Haleston nodded. 'We dare not rest until the brute lies dead beside its fellow.'

The Doctor rolled his eyes to heaven. 'But, your grace, you don't stand a chance!'

At that, Mrs Lunn burst out into helpless sobs, and Teazel barked at the Doctor. Martha wasn't convinced that the dog's bark was worse than his bite. 'Time to go?' she suggested.

'I dare say we're all a little tired and edgy,' Victor said tactfully. 'I'll drive you both back. Thanks awfully for coming here.'

'Sorry there wasn't more we could do,' said Martha. 'Without an X-ray—'

'No X-rays,' Lunn muttered, exhausted.

Martha shrugged. 'If you like, I could check on him again tomorrow.'

'Dr Fenchurch will be here in the morning,' Haleston informed her. 'Thank you all the same, my dear. Good night to you.'

She nodded. Teazel's low growl was all the encouragement she needed to follow the Doctor and Victor from the room. And as Martha went out onto the darkened landing she saw the boy again, hovering in the shadows. She gave him a thumbs-up. He held up his own thumb and smiled before vanishing into the shadows.

'Does Mr Lunn have a son?' she asked casually as they went downstairs.

'Young lad named Ian,' Victor told her. 'Good little urchin. Thirteen or so. Eddie's been so busy of late, agreed to let him come so they could spend a little time together…' He broke off and sighed. 'If you'll excuse me, I'll just creep to the kitchens and chivvy Chivvers along with the first aid essentials. Back in a jiff to play chauffeur.' He walked quickly away, his heels ringing out on the wooden floorboards.

'Funny, you know,' said the Doctor. 'I normally get on very well with dogs.'

'Did the Zygons make that mark on him?' asked Martha quietly.

'They can sting.' The Doctor nodded. 'Sting to stun, maim or kill. And y'know, that's why I think Teazel was barking at me back there – he was taking exception to *this*.' He pulled from his coat pocket a gnarled orange growth. 'He must have recognised the smell. I would say that the same hands that stung Teazel made this. Not *literally* the same hands – although, you never know…'

'Where did you get that?' Martha turned up her nose. 'It looks like… a poo.'

'Organic technology,' said the Doctor. 'It's a kind of homing device, not so much made as *grown*. Tasty bit of kit – well, tasty to Skarasens, anyway. Sends out a signal that says "Eat me, eat me…"'

'I get it,' said Martha. 'So if the Zygons have got something they want mashed, they set off the signal and let their pet monster slip the leash?'

'A Skarasen would tear through anything to get to this.' The Doctor pondered the wizened lump. 'I sneaked this one from out of the teeth of that corpse by the lake.'

'I wondered why you shoved your hand in your pocket after poking about in its mouth.' She looked at him doubtfully. 'So why'd you take it? Souvenir?'

There was a cheeky glint in his eyes. 'Just trying to get on the enemy's wavelength…'

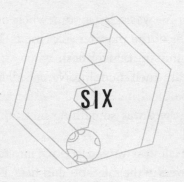

SIX

Haleston sat stiffly in the chair by the window, watching the sunrise. A shaft of bright, peachy light was already warming the room, motes of dust swarming there like flies. The dark corners of the house would slowly lighten. Soon he would hear clanking from the kitchens, the first thump of the house's heartbeat as morning brought it back to life.

He cast an envious look at the mound of starched nightwear and eiderdown that was his sleeping wife. She had snored on, oblivious to Lunn's return, while he hadn't been able to sleep a wink since. He'd written up his journal, although committing the day's strange events to paper had brought him no peace.

He had known Edward Lunn a long time – an upstanding businessman, a loyal friend, a caring husband and father. And now Lunn lay a broken man, while the thing that had broken him – a mockery among

God's creatures – was at large, somewhere out there.

He thought of the monster's corpse at Templewell. The dead chime of its steel flesh when struck by the saw, like a death knell sounding. *Not of Earthly origin*, that Doctor had said.

And now there was something in Lunn's eyes that spoke of hell.

A part of Haleston wanted to crawl into bed and hide under the covers in the safe, soft darkness. But he stood sentinel at the window, knowing the hour to act was ticking closer.

He blinked. There was a speck of colour beside the rill that threaded down the eastern slope of Eskine's peak. It looked like… a tiny figure.

Haleston hesitated for a moment, filled with a nameless dread. Then he raised his binoculars to see.

It was a young girl, her solemn face framed by long, golden curls shining in the sun. Her skinny arm pointed to Wolvenlath Mere. Her eyes seemed fixed on him, as if she knew he was watching her.

Chewing his lip, Haleston lowered the binoculars and rubbed his eyes. 'Ridiculous,' he breathed. 'You can't be seeing things now. A clear gaze, that's what's needed.'

When he raised the glasses again he noticed two things. Firstly, that the girl had gone.

Secondly, that his hands would not stop shaking.

Martha woke groggily at eight that morning. But she

soon came round as the whiff of burning food reached her nostrils. Dressing quickly, she went downstairs and found Monsieur Romand picking at blackened bacon and runny eggs in the dining room.

'Good morning, dear lady,' he said to her.

'Not so far it isn't.' Martha yawned and stretched. 'Have you seen the Doctor?'

'He went out at first light,' said Mrs Unswick, standing in the doorway. The poor woman had been disturbed twice in the night by their going and coming, and her haggard face showed it. 'He said you weren't to worry, and he'd be back later this morning if all was well.'

'Oh,' said Martha, frowning.

'It seems you have been abandoned, my dear, no?' Romand gestured to the seat opposite. 'Perhaps I might entertain you.'

'Happen she'll be more entertained by a good breakfast,' said Mrs Unswick. 'Bacon and eggs do you, Miss Jones?'

'Er, do you have any toast?' she asked.

Mrs U shook her head. 'No bread. Only bacon and eggs, dearie.'

'Then... that'd be great. Thank you.'

The woman bustled away, and Romand lowered his voice confidentially. 'They are not good, but I do not think she can cook anything else at all!'

Martha smiled and sat down opposite. 'So, what have you got planned today?'

'As ever, I search for the story.' He patted his lips with his napkin, smoothing a finger over his trimmed moustache. 'I thought perhaps I might join a hunting expedition with my movie camera, yes? Then, while the plucky Englishmen hunt down their monster, the Frenchman can do some shooting of his own. Who knows! Perhaps I might even capture on film a famous – what is the word – *phantom* of these parts.'

'Like little Molly, you mean?' Sitting here now in streaming sunlight, Martha found it hard to imagine how spooked she had been last night. 'Probably just a girl out playing.'

'Perhaps.' The Frenchman leaned forward over the remains of his breakfast and lowered his voice. 'According to Mrs Unswick, in the village of Beetham there roams a headless hound. It is said he prophesies death for anyone he follows.'

'If he's got no head, how does he know *who* he's following?' Martha pointed out. But mention of a hound had put her in mind of Teazel last night, and her thoughts strayed to his master with the cracked head. *We really should get Mr Lunn's head X-rayed*, she thought idly, *whatever he says*. She remembered the injured man's point-blank refusal…

And then she jumped up from the table.

Romand started in surprise. 'Dear lady, are you unwell?'

'Would you settle for completely stupid?' Realisation was banging her round the head now. The Doctor said that these Zygons could take human form. In which case, Lunn's run-in with them might *really* have left him a changed man. Would alien bones show up on an X-ray? Martha had no idea, but she knew that if *she* were being hunted and a master of disguise, then tricking her way into the company of influential human beings with plenty of guns would be a pretty good bet. But if Lunn *was* a Zygon, how long was he planning to stay undercover? What was he up to there – and how safe were the people around him?

'An English penny for your thoughts,' Romand offered.

'I'll give you some grub for them!' Mrs Unswick announced as she came into the room with a plate of breakfast.

'Thanks, Mrs U,' said Martha. The eggs looked almost raw, and the bacon was charred. She grabbed a rasher anyway and shoved it in her mouth. 'Victor mentioned your garden joins onto the Goldspur estate,' she said with her mouth full. 'Is that right?'

'Very nearly.' Mrs Unswick looked at her uncertainly. 'Though the estate's still a good half-mile distant.'

'I think I should look in on my patient,' she said. She pinched the other bit of bacon to show willing, and smiled. 'Can you point me in the right direction?'

It was a beautiful, clear, crisp morning. The sunlight shimmered on the surface of the lakes, and made even the stubbly remains of the wheat fields glow gold.

The Doctor was hitching a lift in the back of a milk cart, pulled by a sturdy black mare. The milkman was on his way back home now, and passed only a mile or two from the field the TARDIS stood in.

'I'm glad of the company,' he called, and something in his voice told the Doctor he wasn't just being polite. 'Twice this morning I've seen the fetch of poor little Molly Melton. Just standing there in the fields…'

'Oh yes?' The Doctor dangled his legs happily from the back of the cart as it trundled along the rutted lane. 'Pointing, was she?'

'You've seen her too, then. Many folks about here have.' The milkman lowered his voice. 'They say wherever she points is struck by disaster. She's warning souls away. Saving the lives of others now her own's been taken.' He flicked the reins and clicked his tongue, and the mare quickened her step. 'They say she comes to the hunters most of all. Warning them away from the Beast of Westmorland. Urging them to flee while they've got their lives.' He sighed. 'Not that any of them do, of course.'

The Doctor nodded, absently. He was enjoying the clopping of the horse and the squeak of the carriage, the scratchy calls of the larks and terns overhead – and the whirr of his sonic screwdriver. But best of all was the weird, intermittent chitter coming from the decaying lump in his other hand.

'There's life in the old thing yet,' he murmured happily

to himself. 'Dangerous. Verrrrrrry dangerous.'

As if heeding the warning, the control went dead. The Doctor carried on tinkering.

Think, Martha told herself as she marched through the Lodge's overgrown gardens. *You can't just charge in and accuse an invalid of being an alien. But maybe you can find out if the patient's been up to anything unusual in the night, and let the Doctor know when he gets back from wherever he's gone.*

She reached the fence, hitched up her skirt and climbed over into the green slope of the meadow. The grass was long and still wet with the dew despite the sunshine. A few cows watched her warily as she ploughed onward.

The walk took some time. Over the brow of the gentle hill, she could see a high brick wall that signalled the boundary of Goldspur.

Martha was just wondering how she might scale it when the face of a young boy popped into sight at the top of it. He was pale and freckled, with red hair swept back from his forehead. With his aquiline features, he bore a striking resemblance to Edward Lunn. She recognised him at once as the boy she'd seen last night.

'Hello,' he called.

Martha grinned. This could be just the break she'd been hoping for. 'Out playing?'

'Exploring,' the boy corrected her in upper-class tones. 'Old Haleston's grounds are fertile territory.'

'I'm sure they are. You're Ian, aren't you?'

'And you're Miss Martha Jones.' Ian swung himself onto the top of the wall and regarded her. 'I think I shall like you. You helped my father.'

Martha smiled back. 'I'd like to help him some more. How is he this morning?'

'The doctor came to see him…' He must have noticed her reaction. 'Not your Doctor, silly. Dr Fenchurch. Though I much prefer yours.'

'What did Dr Fenchurch say?'

'Not a lot – Father sent him away and gave the tablets he left to Mother…' A cloud crossed Ian's face. 'I think perhaps he hoped they might stop her crying.'

Or else human tranquilisers might affect aliens totally differently, thought Martha.

'Father's very cross he can't remember more about what happened,' Ian went on. 'He shouted at Mother and me when we brought him breakfast… he only calmed down when Lord Haleston left to hunt down whatever he saw at Wolvenlath.'

Martha came to a decision. 'Ian, I think it might be helpful if I paid your father another visit.'

'I'm sure Mother wouldn't mind,' said Ian eagerly. 'But it's too far to walk round. Why not climb the wall? You'll see some of the bricks have been chipped at. Did the job myself last summer, they make perfect footholds.'

'Resourceful,' she commended him, and started to climb.

* * *

The Doctor was striding over field and vale, quoting Wordsworth to cattle at the top of his lungs.

The view was startling from the hillside. Grey crags and bald tors scraped the clouds that dusted the deep blue sky. That blue was reflected in the meres and waters that lay on the land like shards of some great mirror. Fields of grass and rape and barley sat slotted together in green and yellow and copper squares. A charred patch here and there marked the stale seedbeds burned off ready for wheat to be sown.

Heavy footsteps made the Doctor turn. A nearby cow was ambling over, watching him with brown, soulful eyes. It nudged against the side of his leg, pushing at the coat pocket that held the Skarasen control.

'I'm sorry, Daisy, is my alien gadget bothering you?' The Doctor pulled out the Zygon device and shook it. 'Signal keeps stopping and starting. Decomposition in the crystal lattice, most likely...'

Suddenly a thundering, bestial cry sounded in the distance behind him. The cow bolted, and the Doctor turned in time to catch the dark, sleek shape of a Skarasen rise up from a forest in a distant valley. The two humps of its back cleared the treeline, and its head bobbed about on its immensely long neck.

'So you're real, all right,' breathed the Doctor in wonder. 'A second Skarasen, not far from Wolvenlath. Right where Molly Melton said danger would be.'

The Skarasen turned to stare in his direction, and for

a chilling moment the Doctor felt the creature could actually see him, even all the way over there.

'Can you hear it calling?' He waved the signal device in the air. 'Is it a pied piper's flute you have to follow, or a racket you have to shut up before it drives you mad?'

Abruptly, the Skarasen's head ducked back down beneath the treeline. The Doctor frowned at the lump of fungal flesh in his hand, held it to his ear and shook it. 'Stopped again! We need to get you working properly…' He looked over at two more cows, huddled nervously together. 'You know, the thing about organic crystallography is that its atomic structure is quite receptive to sonic vibrations. So if I can find a compatible resonance to heal the transmitter cells…'

He frowned as the cows turned suddenly and ran away.

'Only thinking aloud!' the Doctor called after them.

A throaty, gurgling moan sounded close behind.

And the Doctor turned to find a Zygon bearing down on him, its squashed-up features twisted in rage as its stinging claws reached for his face.

SEVEN

The Doctor recoiled, stuffed the signalling device back in his pocket. Then he grabbed one of the Zygon's wrists with both hands and twisted it hard. The alien hissed with pain, lashed out with its free hand. But the Doctor had staggered back into a fresh-laid cowpat, slippery as a banana skin. Glutinous, claw-like fingers flashed past his eyes as his foot slid from under him, and with a yelp he fell down flat on his back.

'Saved by the bell,' the Doctor panted. 'Well, it *sounds* like a bell, doesn't it? DUNNGGG!'

The Zygon tried to hurl itself on top of him but he lashed out with his slimy foot, catching it a glancing blow to the chest, enough to deflect its fall to the ground beside him.

'What, didn't grasp that little joke?' The Doctor performed two backward rolls to get himself out of the Zygon's range. 'Bit of wordplay, that's very human. You lot should have lessons – idiosyncratic use of language, help you fit in better with the locals. Maybe I could hold a seminar…?'

'You will die,' the Zygon gurgled.

'And that's before I've even told you my fee.' The Doctor feinted back from the stinging claws. 'Killing me is pointless. Not just pointless, it's *stupid*. I mean, here you are, a bunch of Zygons stranded on Earth, ignoring the hand of friendship.' He waggled his left hand in the air. 'Here it is! "Hello!" it says. "Be my friend, Zygons!" it says. And are you listening?'

The Zygon hesitated, wheezing for breath. 'You know of my people.'

The Doctor nodded, his hand still raised. 'And I know that something nasty around here is hurting you and your livestock. It's already killed one of your Skarasens, and last night it mauled one of you to death.' He lowered his hands, held them out imploringly. 'You're vulnerable here. Bullets can stop you. *Humans* can stop you. But I can help you.'

The Zygon stared at him, something like wonder in its eyes.

Then the hatred stole back in.

The Doctor threw himself aside as his attacker lunged forwards, sticky orange fingers clawing for his skin.

'You will give me the trilanic activator,' hissed the Zygon.

'Trilanic activator?' The Doctor looked about for

cover, but aside from a few gorse bushes there was only open ground. 'Oh, you mean your little Skarasen signalling device.' He produced it from his pocket, tossed it in the air and caught it again. 'What's up, worried I'm gonna take control of your mobile food supply? You should be.'

'Return the activator to me,' the Zygon demanded, its voice rasping deeper.

'Nope.' The Doctor backed away, holding the activator up in the air, out of reach. 'Not until you say please.'

The creature glared at him. Then it looked down at the grass.

'Please,' it said.

Lowering his arm, the Doctor stared in disbelief.

'You what?'

'Please.' The Zygon raised its huge, misshapen head. There was something raw, almost desperate in its feral eyes.

'Oh.' The Doctor felt a twinge of guilt for getting its hopes up. 'Well, that's sweet of you to use manners, but no. Like I said, if I can fix this, I might just be able to take control of your Skarasen.' He shook his head sadly. 'What are you lot up to – roaming around the place, trying to kill people like Edward Lunn and his dog... I mean, what's that all about?' The Zygon did not respond, staring back at the ground. 'Or am I wrong? Was it something else that attacked him – the same thing that killed your Skarasen? *Is* it an alien hunter...?'

The Zygon's only answer was to raise its head and charge at him. The Doctor turned and ran in the direction of the TARDIS, and this time he kept running.

The last of the carriages pulled up outside the woods that bordered Wolvenlath Mere. Lord Haleston looked around with grave satisfaction as his guests and friends loaded their guns, and his groundskeeper led the gun dogs from their baskets. Morale was high. A large, dinosaur-like beast had been spotted in the area just this morning – and it hadn't been seen to leave. Already, many of the men were talking keenly of the medals the King would bestow upon whoever bagged the beast.

Haleston sighed. He recalled a happier time, years ago, when the King had hosted a shoot. Just ten of them had killed over 1,300 birds. It had been a glorious day's sport.

There would be no grouse or pheasant in their sights today. This was business, not pleasure. Haleston had squared it with the local authorities and the landowner had given his full cooperation. There were other hunters in the area, and word had it that more were on the way. But Haleston wasn't about to waste time telling them to clear out and leave the job to his party. He was happy to have all hands to the pump. The hunt for the Beast of Westmorland was ready to begin in earnest.

'Whatever's out there, Edward, we'll get it,' Haleston muttered.

He wondered if any of those men had been pointed to Wolvenlath by a lost-looking girl with long, golden hair. He glanced round quickly; half afraid he would glimpse her again. Instead he saw Victor, striding up to him, brandishing his antique blunderbuss.

'What's our plan, old boy?' Victor wondered. 'Give the dogs their head? Fan out and track together to find its lair, or split into smaller parties?'

Haleston regarded him. 'It's most likely that the beast is hiding in the lake. We must fire into the water, attempt to drive it out.'

'And then?'

'Your friend the Doctor was right,' Haleston said slowly. 'The skin of the beast was tougher than steel. If we're to strike this monster down, we must aim for softer parts – the eyes, perhaps.'

'Good thinking.' Victor nodded. 'If we can blind the thing it should be less of a threat.'

Perhaps, thought Haleston. Then he tried to bury the doubt as deep as it would go. 'We need to consider how we can contain the brute once we've roused it from its lair… A pit, perhaps?' He sighed and shook his head wearily. 'But no, one can't forget the sheer size of the thing. It would take weeks to dig such a hole, we couldn't possibly…' He tailed off as, to his surprise, a sly smile began to spread over Victor's face. 'Whatever's the matter with you?'

'Lord Haleston,' Victor announced, 'I think perhaps

I know where I can lay my hands on the very answer to your prayers…'

Shoes gripped in one hand, Martha jumped down from the wall. She landed in the huge pile of springy leaves Ian had plucked and gathered together for just such a purpose. The landing still jarred through her ankles, but it was fine.

Ian was already down and waiting for her. She caught the admiring look in his clear blue eyes and smiled.

'Perfectly done,' he told her, a faint blush coming to his pale, freckled cheeks. 'You're not at all like a proper grown up.'

'Thank you. I think.' She picked herself up and slipped on her shoes. 'Believe it or not, in my family they think of me as the mature one.' A thought struck her. 'Speaking of proper grown-ups, won't anyone be wondering where you are?'

'Mother said I was allowed to play outside today, so there was nothing Nanny could do to stop me,' Ian smiled. But we'd better tread carefully in any case and hope nobody sees us. I'm bound to get into trouble for smuggling someone in over the wall.'

'Now you tell me!' said Martha, feeling more like a naughty kid every second.

Ian led Martha through the amazing grounds, past towering topiaries and ornamental pools. 'We'll get in through the conservatory,' he explained. 'From there we'll trot along the passage to the front door. Then we can pretend you've called in the proper manner.'

He led her round to the conservatory's elegant wooden door and opened it soundlessly. Once inside, Ian directed her to stand behind a large rubber plant. 'I'll go first and check the way is clear. It should be. All the men are out on the hunt, and the ladies will be taking tea and gassing in the drawing room. All except Mother, who's lying down upstairs.'

Martha felt a twinge of guilt as she waited for him. To Ian all this was a great game, but she knew it might end with her unmasking his father as a monster.

'All right, this way,' said Ian, beckoning her onwards out into a long, airy passageway. A large window lit one end, and a sharp turn to the right hid the other end from view. 'If we're spotted—'

He broke off as the heavy clunk of a door opening sounded from around the corner.

'Get out of sight!' Ian whispered. He tried the handle on the large door beside him. 'It's unlocked. Quick!' He opened the door so she could tumble inside, then pulled it back shut behind her.

First, Martha caught a whiff of iron in the air. Then a cry caught in her throat as she saw something standing behind the mahogany desk, holding a large leather-bound book. The figure was tall, red-orange and bulky. A thick, puckered scar ran through its left eye all the way down to its chest, doing nothing to enhance its brutal looks.

'Uh-oh,' she said.

The Zygon hurled the diary at her face. She raised her hands to deflect it, but as she backed away she stumbled over a chair and fell against the wall. The next thing she heard was a thick crack and the shatter of breaking glass. Turning, she watched as the alien pushed its way out through the window and ran.

The door to the office opened and Ian appeared. 'I heard the…' He looked dumbfounded between her face and the window. 'Good grief, Martha…'

'It wasn't me. Someone was already in here, going through Lord Haleston's desk.' Martha grabbed the diary and got to her feet. 'They saw me and took off.'

Ian stared at her, wide-eyed. 'I wondered why the door wasn't locked!'

'But why would that thing care what Lord Haleston's been writing about?' She crossed to the window but there was no one in sight, so she flicked through the diary. Page after page was filled with meticulously neat handwriting. 'Can't imagine it's planning to crash one of his society dos… So what does it want to know?'

'It? What do you mean, Martha? Who was here?'

'I'm not sure.' For a moment she considered chasing after the thing. Then she realised she might just have a way to test her theory. 'Come on, Ian. Let's check on your father.'

'Yes,' Ian decided. 'He'll know what to do.'

Martha nodded. *And if he's not in his bed, then I'll know I was right.* 'Who opened the door out there in the passage, anyway?'

'It was probably Chivvers,' said Ian. 'No one came though – and worst luck, too, because if I'd had some back-up I could have dived in and saved you.'

'Thanks, Ian,' said Martha, sticking her head out into the corridor. 'Maybe next time I—'

'What is the meaning of this?' came a booming voice.

Startled, Martha turned to find a thin, mean-looking woman in a starched grey uniform standing in the conservatory doorway, hands on hips. Her piercing blue eyes shone accusingly – and if there had been any milk about, then the woman's pinched, twisted features would have curdled it in seconds.

'Nanny Flock,' squeaked Ian.

'You've come from the garden,' Martha realised. 'Did you see anyone?'

Nanny Flock did nothing to disguise the sneer on her face. 'I don't answer to the likes of you.'

'What were you doing out there?' Martha persisted.

The woman's glare fell on Ian. 'This nasty little limb should be playing outside. So I go to check he's not getting up to mischief, and what do I find? He's smuggling undesirables into the house and breaking windows.'

'That's not it!' Martha tried to stay calm. 'There was an intruder in here, we surprised them.'

Nanny Flock ignored her, smiling smugly at Ian. 'Oh, your mother will be hearing all about this.'

'Good idea,' said Martha, turning on her heel, grabbing Ian by the hand and setting off quickly down the passage. 'In fact, I think we should tell his father first. Right now.'

Nanny Flock gasped. 'How dare you walk away from me!'

Easy, Martha thought, quickening her step. *Because if Lunn's not in his bedroom, he's the Zygon – and you don't matter one bit. And if he is there, then you could be the Zygon. And I'm not about to let you prove it with Ian here.*

'Come back at once!' the woman cried.

Ian looked up at Martha. 'We're going to be in so much trouble!' She saw a scandalised smile spread slowly over his face. 'This is the most exciting day I can remember!'

'And it's not over yet,' Martha told him, trying to smile back as she hurried up the stairs.

She hesitated outside Lunn's room, and Ian knocked. 'Father? It's Ian, and the lady who nursed you last night.' He swallowed hard. 'May we come in?'

There was no reply. Martha could hear brisk footsteps on the stairs. They didn't have long. Taking a deep breath, Martha's hand closed around the ivory handle and opened the door.

EIGHT

Martha peered into the gloomy room. The closed velvet drapes billowed inwards in a gust of wind, casting a halo of light around Edward Lunn. He lay in bed, apparently fast asleep, his head to one side.

A rush of relief went through her – until she realised nothing had changed. Who was to say there weren't *two* Zygons in the house, that Lunn hadn't sneaked downstairs and invited his buddies to hide indoors?

'Ian, whatever are you doing?'

The voice was quiet and brittle. Martha turned to find Mrs Lunn was standing behind her. The woman's pale skin seemed more bleached out than ever thanks to the ivory silk kimono she wore.

'Sorry, Mother,' said Ian, as Martha pulled the door closed. 'Only there was an intruder in the house, and we were worried—'

'The only intruder around here is *her*, ma'am.' Nanny

Flock had arrived on the scene, pointing a bony finger at Martha. 'She forced her way in through a window downstairs.'

'That wasn't me,' Martha began calmly. 'I met Ian playing outside, and wondered if your husband was any better.'

'She's after the silver, I'll be bound,' the nanny sniped.

'Martha's a friend of Victor Meredith's,' Ian protested. 'She's not a thief!'

'This impertinence is disgraceful, Ian. I will not tolerate it.' Mrs Lunn glared at her son. 'Go to your room, I will speak with you later.'

Martha watched Ian troop reluctantly away. 'It wasn't his fault, you know,' she said quietly.

'I do not wish to hear any more of this,' snapped Mrs Lunn. 'My husband is in the care of a proper doctor now and we no longer require your services, Miss Jones.'

The doorbell rang. Teazel started barking furiously downstairs, and Mrs Lunn closed her eyes wearily. 'Miss Flock, kindly inform Chivvers about the broken window, and let him decide what to do.'

'Very good, ma'am.' The nanny inclined her head. 'What about the lad?'

Mrs Lunn shook her head. 'I'll deal with him myself.'

Feeling helpless, angry and humiliated, Martha turned and marched away down the steps to the main hall. Chivvers was just answering the door. It was Claude Romand.

'I wish to accompany the hunting party,' Romand announced grandly, setting his tweed cap at a jaunty angle. 'To record it for both the public and for posterity, yes?'

'Too late,' said Martha, striding out past Chivvers before he could open his mouth to reply. 'The hunting party's already off hunting.' She linked arms with Romand and led him back down the steps. 'Though if it's monsters they're after they should have stayed here.'

'Not a good visit?' Romand enquired.

'As good as Mrs U's breakfast,' she agreed. Then she clocked his motor car. It was burgundy, less sporty-looking than Victor's and roomier, with a canvas roof and a ROVER badge on the front grille. 'Claude, did you see anything odd in the gardens on your way up here?'

'Nothing,' he informed her.

'Figures.' She sighed. 'I only hope the Doctor gets back soon.'

'He *is* back!' The Doctor suddenly popped up into view from his repose on the back seat with a big grin on his face. 'Hello!'

Martha felt a rush of relief. 'Doctor! Where the hell have you been?'

'Oh, picking up some bits and bobs, smelling the flowers, talking to cows. Hot-footing it across the countryside as if my very life depended on it – which it did, of course… Monsieur Romand spotted me down the lane as he was turning into Goldspur, and not a moment too soon. Look, blisters the size of my toes!' He stuck a bare foot out through the rear window and looked at her meaningfully. 'A lot of *orange* around at this time of year…'

'Tell me about it,' said Martha with a shudder. 'No, hang on, before you do…' She ran to the car, climbed over some camera gear to get into the back seat beside him and squeezed his hand. 'Let's just have a moment.'

He squeezed her hand back and gave her another big smile. 'A moment,' he agreed.

Romand dropped them at the end of the lane that led to the Lodge, then rattled away in pursuit of the hunt. Martha and the Doctor – who was now sporting a new pair of plimsolls – took the walk leisurely, yet wasted no time recounting their different adventures.

'By the time I'd hightailed it all the way to the TARDIS there was no sign of anyone following,' the Doctor said, concluding his own account. 'And the journey back as far as Goldspur was quiet too. A couple of cows got quite excited to see me, but that's nothing new…'

'How many of these Zygons can there be in the area?' asked Martha. 'I mean, if I see one here and you see one there…?'

'Tricky to say.' The angular lines of the Doctor's face were drawn sharper in a frown. 'Could be just a well-informed handful. Or there could be hundreds and they've taken over everybody in the area.'

Martha looked appalled. 'Does that mean that all the *real* people would be dead?'

'No, the Zygons have to keep their victims alive,' the Doctor explained. 'They need to update their body prints quite frequently, or they revert to their true form.'

'Isn't there any way to spot them?' asked Martha.

'Sometimes they come across as a bit surly, a bit cold,' he said. 'But generally they're pretty good at what they do – which is stay hidden.' He threw his arms up crossly in the air. 'And that's what I don't understand. If someone's hunting them down, why aren't they lying low, tucked away in their secret spaceship?'

'Maybe their spaceship's been discovered,' Martha suggested. 'Or destroyed. Couldn't you check for... I dunno, spaceship particle fallout or whatever?'

He gave her a funny look. 'Spaceship particle fallout?'

Martha shrugged. 'Well, a blown-up spaceship's got to leave some trace behind, hasn't it?'

Now the Doctor grinned. 'Good thinking. And exactly what I did when I went back to the TARDIS.'

She cuffed him round the shoulder in mock reproach. 'And?'

'Nothing! Diddly squat. Fat zilch. Not even the local atomic disturbance you'd pick up from a recently landed spaceship.'

'So either the Zygon-hunters have been here a long time like the Zygons themselves,' Martha reasoned, 'or else they're shielded from the TARDIS's ropy old scanners…'

'Oi!'

'… or else there *are* no hunters.' Martha looked at him. 'They don't exist.'

'Something took the head off that Skarasen and did for that Zygon we found in the road,' the Doctor reminded her. 'And as for his mates, well, they're acting very oddly.'

Martha nodded. 'Sneaking into houses to read people's diaries…'

'And the Zygon who said please. Sounds like the title of a book, doesn't it? *The Little Zygon Who Said Please*. What a book that'd be! I'd break into someone's house myself to read that…'

Martha interrupted him. 'Was it sweet-talking you because it wanted something in particular?'

'It wanted that trilanic activator I found.' The Doctor produced the funny lump from his pocket. 'I think it saw me start to summon its Skarasen…'

'What, you used that thing like a dog whistle?'

He nodded thoughtfully. 'I was tinkering around. Somehow got it to transmit a bit on a wavelength our elusive Skarasen responds to.'

Martha put on a spooky voice. 'Maybe the ghost of Molly Melton was giving you a hand from the spirit world.'

'Sounds like she's very obliging with her appearances,'

the Doctor mused. 'People all over the Lakes have seen her warning people away from trouble spots. Even the milkman.'

'But she's not really a ghost, is she?' said Martha. 'I mean… she's got to be a Zygon, right?'

'The idea of taking a human form is to blend in, not draw attention to yourself,' said the Doctor. 'Perhaps someone else is putting her up to this…'

'Who?'

'Dunno.' The Doctor puffed out his cheeks as they strolled up to the front door. 'Nothing seems to add up, no one story seems to fit.'

Martha tried the door and frowned. 'It's locked.'

She reached for the bell-pull but the Doctor had already whipped out the sonic. The tip of the ceramic wand whirred and glowed blue, and the door clicked open. He smiled at her. 'Shame to disturb Mrs U—'

'Who's there?' came a frightened shout from upstairs.

'Only us,' called the Doctor, his face creasing in concern. Martha joined him as he rushed upstairs. 'Everything all right?'

Mrs Unswick came out onto the gloomy landing looking a little flustered. 'Oh, my dears, you did surprise me. I thought I'd locked the door. With all this talk of a beast and the sightings of young Molly, well…'

Martha heard the ticking, flickering sound of a projector coming from Romand's room. 'I thought Mr Romand was out?'

The woman gave a sheepish smile. 'You've caught me in the act, I'm afraid. I wasn't expecting anyone back so soon, and the police will be calling to collect the film later this morning. I didn't think Monsieur Romand would mind…'

The Doctor walked past her and opened the door. Romand's projector was set up, casting its blurred black-and-white footage of the Kelmore aftermath on the bare wall.

'It's just incredible, isn't it?' Mrs Unswick went on. 'You can watch real people moving about, even when the house is empty.' A faraway look came into her eyes as she stared at the wall. 'I mean, look at them… they're a little like ghosts themselves, aren't they? Sort of here, but not…'

Martha nodded politely. She'd forgotten how incredible a technological breakthrough like this must seem to someone from this time – until recently, a photo was as high-tech as it got. She imagined showing Mrs U the Sugababes video she'd downloaded to her mobile a few weeks back. *Maybe not*, she decided.

'Let's watch it together from the start, shall we?' After some poking about at the projector, she got the film to run backwards.

'Hang about,' said the Doctor, pointing to the screen. 'What's that?'

'What's what?' While Martha squinted at the blurry image of a smashed-in mansion, the Doctor crossed to the projector and started flicking switches and levers like an expert. First the film stopped, then it spun forwards again. 'Doctor…?'

'There.' With a steel *shunk!* the image was held trembling on the wall. It showed a barn in the background of the debris of the grand house, a barn with its front door wide open, showing off the hazy shapes inside. 'Bit of focusing…' His nimble fingers spun a wheel on the side of the projector and sharpened the image.

Now Martha could make out something that looked like a big funnel in a framework of pipes. 'So what are we looking at?'

The Doctor donned his glasses and peered at the glowing image. 'That thing in front looks like a double cylinder hoisting engine.'

'Gracious!' Mrs Unswick exclaimed. 'A what?'

'Lifting gear,' he said, glancing at Martha. 'Kind of an early crane.'

Martha shrugged. 'So?'

'So that's pretty specialist lifting equipment. Funny thing to find parked in the Lord of the Manor's barn.'

'That's Sir Albert and Lady Morton's residence,' said Mrs Unswick.

'He was Victor's client, wasn't he?' Martha recalled.

'I know he died when the Beast ran rampant.' Mrs Unswick turned from the screen. 'Wonder what he was doing with all that new-fangled machinery.'

'So do I,' murmured the Doctor. He crossed to the

windows and swept open the curtains. 'How far is Kelmore from here, Mrs U?'

'Five miles or so,' she informed him.

'Five miles?' Martha was afraid she knew what was coming next. 'That's a long walk.'

'But it's not such a long ride,' Mrs U told her, her haggard face brightening with a smile. 'Did I neglect to show you the stables?'

'Ha!' cried the Doctor with delight. 'Kelmore on horseback – here we come!'

NINE

The bedroom at Goldspur was cool and dark. Two creatures stood inside it, watching the prone figure of Edward Lunn as he slept.

They were Zygons in their natural forms.

'How do the humans know of our kind, Commander?' hissed one, smaller than its superior and with a green-orange tinge to its skin.

'It does not matter, Algor,' said the commander; a massive Zygon with a scarred face, his name was Brelarn. 'The Doctor and his friend are outsiders, not trusted by this community of primitive fools. Talk of aliens will not be heeded. Martha Jones knows this, or she would have made explicit what she saw in Haleston's study.'

'But Haleston must know the Skarasen is not native to this world?'

'His journals betray his fear of what he cannot understand.' Brelarn's lips twitched in what might have been a smile. 'Haleston seeks to create a disturbance in the waters of Wolvenlath, in the hope of rousing the Skarasen from hiding. Your assessment of this plan?'

'Given the Skarasen's present condition,' Algor said cautiously, 'they may be able to disturb it. But then they must subdue it.'

Brelarn nodded. 'By now, Haleston will have been told of the construction machinery…'

'The Doctor and the female have already left for Kelmore,' Algor informed him. 'They will discover it also.' He hissed, a low, threatening noise. 'This Doctor is dangerous.'

'And yet, he may be of great value to us,' Brelarn told him. 'See that our field troops maintain constant watch on the Doctor's progress.'

'Our troops near exhaustion, Commander,' warned Algor. 'Morale is low. Some feel your strategy is based on unacceptable levels of risk—'

'I am Warlord of the Zygons,' rasped Brelarn, bearing down on Algor, 'and if our people are to survive and triumph and refashion this world in the image of our own, then calculated risks *must* be taken.' The intensity in his eyes faded, and his breathing became a little heavier. 'These are difficult times. But they are filled with unique opportunities. Opportunities which must be taken…'

A look of understanding passed between the two creatures. Then, the air seemed to shimmer and burn around the Zygons' monstrous forms as they prepared to blend back into the world of humans.

As she followed Mrs Unswick and the Doctor out to the stables, Martha noticed a large, black carriage standing in the courtyard. 'Couldn't we take that?' she asked. 'Comfier than horseback.'

'I'm afraid not,' said Mrs Unswick. 'I let a friend of mine keep it here, but he's collecting it later...' She stopped and held her stomach.

'Feeling all right?' asked the Doctor.

'I fear I'm a little unsettled by the cinema show,' she said, smiling weakly. 'Would you mind tacking up yourself?'

'No problem!' said the Doctor cheerily.

'Why not go and have a lie down,' Martha suggested.

'Thank you,' said Mrs Unswick. She looked pale and unwell. 'Oh, and you'd better leave the black horse be. He won't be ridden. Doesn't like strangers.' She forced a smile. 'Do excuse me.' And with that, the matronly woman shuffled off back inside.

'How do we even find the stables?' Martha wondered.

The Doctor sniffed. 'Just follow our noses.'

He was right. Martha was no expert, but reckoned the landlady's three horses had been left untended for a little too long. They looked well fed, but their tails were tangled and their flanks were covered with stable stains. And, judging from the mushrooms growing in the corners of the smelly stable, they definitely hadn't been mucked out for a while. The black one snapped at Martha when she tried to pat its neck, so she and the Doctor decided to heed Mrs U's advice and go for the others.

Once back outside in the fresh air, Martha watched the Doctor move easily and confidently around the horses, feeling more than a little nervous. She'd loved ponies as a kid, but wasn't exactly experienced at riding them.

But as they set off together, her limited knowledge started to come back. And, luckily, her chosen horse – a chestnut gelding with calm, dark eyes – proved to be well schooled and to have a forgiving temperament. She supposed he was quite used to different riders. Aside from once almost throwing her off when he pulled his head down to graze on the long grass growing at the side of the muddy lane, he gave her a surprisingly pleasant journey through the countryside. He had a long stride and walked out with his ears pricked, responding obediently to her hesitant aids.

The Doctor rode beside her on a dark bay horse with a black tail that he'd christened Arthur. In fact, for some reason he'd christened *all* the horses Arthur.

'So why are we going to Kelmore, then?' Martha enquired.

'There's something in the air,' came the evasive reply. 'At least, I'm hoping there is.'

'Probably the whiff of those stables,' said Martha sourly. 'Mrs U can't have cleaned out Arthur, Arthur and

Arthur in a while. It's cruel. I mean, I know there must be a lot to do when you're running your own place, but even so...' She frowned. 'You'd think she'd have got some more help in since Clara left...'

'Me and Hercules could have used some help that time we had to clean out the Augean stables in a single day,' the Doctor announced. He had pulled out the mouldy old Zygon activator from his pocket and was turning it idly in his fingers. 'You know, as part of his twelve labours. Muck everywhere. You couldn't move for the stuff.'

Martha sensed a wind-up. 'What, you helped Hercules from the Greek myths?'

'Be serious! As if that could ever happen!' He peered more closely at the orange lump. 'No, this was on the *planet* Augea. Luckily, a day there is the same as three months on Earth. We finished in bags of time and had a big picnic. I do love a picnic... Mind you, we had to muck out the dreaded Cerberus afterwards, which wasn't so easy. Wasn't just heads he had three of, let me tell you...'

As the lanes and the tall tales meandered on, the muscles in Martha's legs and back began to protest against the long ride. But at last they passed a sign proclaiming the boundary of Kelmore.

Not that they needed telling. The churned-up earth and splintered trees by the roadside were advertisement enough. Martha's Arthur snorted and stopped dead as if spooked. She clicked her tongue and touched him with her heels. Tossing up his head, he stepped backwards.

'Steady,' she said, shortening her reins.

'Whoa, boy!' the Doctor cried to his own Arthur. He turned him round, rode back to Martha and held up his activator. 'I think they can hear this.'

Martha stroked her horse's neck, trying to calm him as faint trembles of eerie alien song pulsated from the Zygon device. 'It's started signalling. Why?'

'Told you something was in the air. Around here, anyway.' The Doctor turned to her and grinned. 'Diastellic transmissions. They leave a trace resonance in the airwaves – can last for a good couple of weeks.' He tapped the activator. 'And those traces are stimulating regrowth in the organic crystals since they were generated by a similar device.'

Martha found her horse edging closer to the Doctor's for comfort. 'In which case, the Skarasen that trashed Kelmore was summoned here. And if you've got that activator signalling again, aren't we going to have some pretty unpleasant company on the way?'

'Oh, shouldn't think so.' The activator went dead, and the Doctor smiled. 'You know the way your mobile beeps when you plug it in to charge it up? I think that was the same thing. It'll be regenerating its cells now... But it shouldn't actually start transmitting till it's properly triggered.'

'Which you can do with the sonic.' She widened her eyes at him. 'Then what?'

'Aha! *Then* all I need to do is find a way of keeping the Beast of Westmorland docile long enough to reprogram it. Convince it that Skarasens really love the Arctic Circle, safely out the way.' The Doctor grinned. 'And if the Zygons want to keep getting their fix of lactic fluid, they'll have to go out there with it. Good big place to hide, the Arctic. No one else around to get hurt. Problem solved.'

'We hope,' Martha murmured.

Ian's anger had died down into boredom. He was fed up of sitting in his room, waiting for his mother to remember she was supposed to be talking to him.

Now Father's been hurt she ought to turn to me, Ian thought. But no, she just stayed in her room, lying down with one of her headaches. And meanwhile, it was only a matter of time before Nanny Flock came in with the usual punishment – an extra large spoonful of castor oil emptied over his tongue…

He was gloomily contemplating the thought when he heard Teazel barking outside – frantic, aggressive barks.

The intruder, Ian thought with a thrill of fear.

He ran over to the open window and saw Teazel standing motionless on the lawn beneath, as if getting a scent. He cursed. If only he could get down there, Teazel could lead him straight to the intruder. The scoundrel would surrender soon enough with the Mastiff's jaws around his leg, and Ian would be able to show his mother and nanny that he and Martha had been telling the truth right along.

Teazel glanced up and saw him. He barked once as if in recognition – or in warning. But now Ian had noticed the thick ivy that smothered the wall from the ground to the window. It must have been growing there for decades, securing itself ever more tightly to the stone. If he scrambled down, spider-like and swift…

'He who hesitates is lost,' Ian told himself, and swung himself down from the window sill, sinking his hands into lustrous leaves and snaking creepers as he clambered down the green-clad brickwork. The moment he touched the ground, feeling slightly giddy with fear and exhilaration, he looked around to check his escape had not been observed. There was no one in sight. But now Teazel was heading off through the gardens.

'Lead on, boy,' whispered Ian and, with a thumping heart, ran after him.

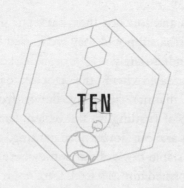

TEN

As Martha let her horse lead her along the churned-up road, a creeping feeling of déjà vu turned her spine to ice. It was like being inside Romand's flickering film show, only living colour made everything so much worse. The sense of trauma still hung in the air. Houses lay demolished, carts crushed, as if invisible elephants had fallen from the sky. She watched people dressed in mourning black cluster outside the roofless church. The graveyard was littered with the crumbs of shattered tombstones.

It wasn't long before she and the Doctor had coaxed their horses up to Morton Manor. One corner of the house had been demolished, and a couple of thickset men were sifting through possessions scattered about the tumble of masonry. Another was heaving a huge chunk of fallen hedge across the trench-torn battleground of the front lawn. They glanced at the new arrivals and touched their hats, but showed little interest. Martha supposed they were used to strangers poking about here lately.

'Splendid day, what?' the Doctor called in an aristocratic manner, jumping down from Arthur. 'Any chance of rustling up the ostler? Lady Morton's expecting us and our horses need parking.'

'Jack the stable-boy's about somewhere, sir,' one of the men informed him. 'I'll fetch him.'

The Doctor nodded approvingly. 'Where's her ladyship staying, with the house in this state?'

'In the guest cottage, sir,' said the red-faced man pulling the hedge. 'But I'm afraid she can't receive you now. She's "otherwise engaged".' He said the words carefully, like he'd been taught them parrot-fashion.

'That's all right,' the Doctor said, helping Martha down from her horse. 'We're only here to inspect the machines.'

Disapproving looks passed between the men. 'Top barn's over that way, backs onto the canal.'

'Splendid.' The Doctor strode away across the lawn, linking arms with Martha. 'There we are! See? Oh, yes. Act like you own the place, can't go wrong.'

'But we *don't* own the place, do we? We're trespassing!'

'Only in a physical sense,' he said defensively.

'A canal next to a lake,' said Martha, noticing the beautiful view beyond the gardens. 'This district really does like to hog the water, doesn't it?'

'Useful to get about,' the Doctor remarked. 'For humans by boat… or Skarasens by flipper.'

Soon they had reached the barn. The canal stretched past its rear doors like a flat, grey strip, and a kind of makeshift jetty had been built there. Around the front, the broken door on show in Romand's film had been removed completely, and the Doctor waltzed inside to study the heavy-duty machinery. It was like some museum exhibit to Martha, depicting the early tools of the construction game. Several more large crates were stacked high at the rear, not yet opened.

The Doctor threw loving looks in all directions. 'What a haul! Locomotive crane, American ditcher…' He hugged a hydraulic arm protruding from one of the machines, then, with a grating noise, acted out the opening and closing of the colossal claw dangling from another.

Martha raised her eyebrows. 'What does this stuff actually do?'

'Well, this one is for digging ditches along rail-beds, that one's a general-purpose excavator. And look at this, one of the first travelling derricks! Movable, pivoted arm…' The Doctor clicked his tongue happily. 'Could shift some serious weight, this could. All this stuff must have cost a fortune.' He scooped some papers from the floor. 'And according to the delivery note, it was transported from Sheffield by barge… the day before the Skarasen attacked this place.'

'Those wacky English upper classes,' said Martha. 'They hide away tons of machinery that could clear the damage to the manor in hours, and let the peasants toil to clear it by hand instead.'

'Perhaps no one knows how to use it. I mean, instruction manuals are all well and good, but when your average farm worker can't read...' The Doctor frowned and pulled a face. 'Wonder what Sir Albert wanted with all this lot.'

Martha shrugged. 'Does it matter?'

'Maybe not,' he said, still lost in thought. 'I'd like to know though, just the same. Shame her ladyship's otherwise engaged, or we could ask her. Tell you what! Let's ask her anyway!' And, with that, the Doctor launched himself like a pinstriped missile, out through the door and down the path towards her ladyship's quaint little red-brick cottage.

Martha jogged to catch up with him – and almost cannoned into the back of him when he suddenly stopped. Like him, she saw a slightly crumpled, very familiar motor car was parked outside the cottage – and then Victor came out through the front door.

'Well, bless me!' he declared, with a wonky smile. 'Doctor, Miss Jones, whatever are you doing here?'

'Oh, just passing,' said the Doctor airily. 'Thought we'd drop in on the Lady of the house, take some tea, p'raps a biscuit or two...'

'And then ask her why she's got about a hundred tons

of construction gear in that barn over there,' Martha concluded.

The Doctor nodded. 'And then ask *you*, how come you're chatting to her ladyship behind closed doors when you should be off hunting monsters?'

'I believe I told you I had business here,' Victor informed him, looking genuinely affronted. 'Happily, my visit to Lady Morton is not simply as lawyer or friend, but as an emissary of Lord Haleston – here to conduct some business that will benefit us all.'

The Doctor smiled. 'Do tell, old boy.'

Victor regarded the Doctor haughtily for a few moments. Then he shrugged. 'To answer your earlier question, I have no idea why Sir Albert decided to move into the construction business, particularly when buying that machinery damned near bankrupted him. But I may have found a rather more colourful use for his equipment.' He smiled and tapped his nose. 'I've made arrangements to have it all transported to Wolvenlath, right away.'

Martha's eyes widened. 'You think you can use that stuff to capture the Skarasen?'

Victor frowned. 'It's the Beast of Westmorland we're after, m'dear! And after a good search of the woods, we came across eyewitnesses who actually saw it submerge in Wolvenlath Mere.'

'I think I might have been one of them,' the Doctor murmured. 'Go on.'

'Well, one of the chaps served with the Royal Miners and Sappers, and he's got a pile of diving gear – suit, pump and twelve-bolt helmet. We can take it in turns to probe the secrets of the mere, find the blessed thing's watery lair…' Victor was quite flushed with excitement. 'That achieved, we simply excavate a suitably big pit, rouse the Beast from its slumbers, and drive it into the hole with heavy gunfire.'

The Doctor looked horrified. 'You know, ordinarily I'm quite good with wild, insanely improvised plans with no thought for personal safety. But *this*, Victor… this is off the scale. That thing will kill all of you.'

'Not so!' Victor lowered his voice confidentially. 'Lady Morton informs me there are crates full of wire rope and heavy-duty chains stored in that barn too. We can pin the Beast to the ground. Old Haleston even says he'll hire the gear, so Lady M will receive much-needed funds. It's a gift! It's… fate!'

'Or *fatal*,' said the Doctor, hands thrust into his coat pockets, as deep as they would go. 'By the way, was Claude Romand filming your lot this morning?'

'Yes, he tracked us down in the end,' said Victor, grinning. 'Singled me out for a shot of my own, said I cut quite a dashing figure.'

'Martha needs to see him urgently.'

Martha reacted. 'I do?'

'You do!' the Doctor agreed. 'So Victor, could you take her back to Wolvenlath with you?'

'I've no idea if he's still there, and it's certainly not the safest place for a young filly to be…' Victor smiled. 'But how could I resist a drive in the sunshine with so pleasant a companion?'

Martha waited till he'd crossed to the crank handle at the front of the car before pretending to make herself sick. She drew close to the Doctor and spoke in a low voice. 'What urgent business? What're you playing at?'

'Oh, don't worry about your horse,' he said. 'I'll persuade Jack the stable-boy to put him up in comfort here for a bit.' He pulled some crisp, large notes from his pocket. 'See? Took some money from the TARDIS. Right year and everything. Oh, yeah! Don't say I can't do practical.'

'But why aren't *you* coming?'

He shrugged. 'The activator's still recharging. Could take another few hours, at least. I need to use that time to try and adapt it. See if I can use it not only to summon the Skarasen, but to plant suggestions in its little cyborg brain.'

Martha nodded. 'Suggestions like "Clear off and don't come back". But why can't I stay with you? What does Claude have to do with anything?'

'He's just an excuse,' the Doctor muttered. 'I want you to gatecrash the hunting party and do anything you can to break it up.'

'What, say I've seen Bigfoot round the corner, hide their diving gear, that sort of thing?'

But the Doctor wasn't smiling. 'Those men are playing with fire, not water. If the Skarasen's hiding in that lake, the Zygon ship could be hidden there too. Provoke them, and…'

'Things could get messy,' said Martha with a shudder.

He nodded. 'On the other hand, if I come galloping along on Arthur with the power to command the Skarasen, there'll be no killer cyborg milk-cow to worry about – and if the Zygons want their food supply back, they'll have to listen to my terms.' The Doctor looked at her urgently. 'But I must have some time.'

'Ready, my dear?' Victor called, turning up the collars of his motoring jacket.

'I'll do all I can,' Martha told the Doctor. She climbed into the car beside Victor, and just managed a quick wave goodbye before they sped away down the driveway.

Martha had hoped to avoid driving with Victor again. At least Romand took things quite slowly in his Rover. Victor seemed to revel in taking the turns as quickly as possible, and while she was keen to be out of the car as soon as possible, that didn't involve flying out through the windscreen.

They had gone a good few miles when Martha suddenly glimpsed movement through the high hedges in the field beyond.

A cluster of orange bodies. A wagon hurtling over heather moorland.

'Victor, stop the car,' she shouted.

But he was already braking. He'd seen it too. Once the car had stopped, they both jumped out and pushed awkwardly through the brambly hedge.

'Good Lord!' breathed Victor.

Martha muttered something more colourful under her breath. A terrified-looking black horse with no rider was charging towards them, pulling a carriage that rattled and shook as it bounced over the uneven ground. With a shiver, she recognised it as the carriage she'd seen at the Lodge. Three Zygons clung to the carriage, one attacking the roof, the others tugging on the door as if trying to get inside. Two more were running over the moorland in pursuit.

It was a surreal scene, and it rooted Martha to the spot. The horse's ears were flat against its head, its hide strafed with stings and scurf. She realised it was the horse that had snapped at her in Mrs U's stables. And it was showing no signs of getting any friendlier.

Horse, carriage and Zygons were heading straight for her and Victor.

ELEVEN

Martha grabbed hold of Victor's hand. 'Move!' she shouted. She dragged him back through the tangled hedgerow, the pounding of hooves growing louder all the time. 'Get in the car!'

Victor scrambled into the front and Martha dived in the back – as, with a splintering crash, the horse ploughed through the hedgerow and the carriage tried to follow. But it couldn't. It jammed hard against the dense foliage, tipped over. The horse's neck snapped back as the reins came up tight. Martha closed her eyes but couldn't block the animal's scream or the heavy thud of its body smashing into the carriage.

Then a loud, metallic thump jolted through Martha as the body of a Zygon bashed down onto the bonnet of the Opel. The creature, thrown clear of the carriage by the collision, raised the fleshy dome of its head and gave a chilling, guttural roar.

Victor scrambled into the back beside Martha. But the Zygon seemed uninterested. Its two mates were lying unmoving in the road, but it didn't bother with them either. It turned back to the carriage – now lying mangled on its side in the hedge with one of its wheels missing – and stepped over the prone body of the horse. Then it started tugging again on the door. The two others she'd seen pursuing the carriage across the field were still advancing, more slowly now.

Victor was white-faced. 'What are those things?'

'Determined,' breathed Martha. She took a deep, shaky breath. 'Who's in the coach anyway? Mrs Unswick said a friend of hers was collecting it…'

'Not much we can do. We'd better hot-foot it.' Victor bunched his fists as the Zygon reached in through the carriage window. 'If only I had my eight-bore!'

But suddenly a huge, terrifying dog burst through the hedgerow on the other side of the road, its jaws bared. Martha saw the swelling on its back and realised it was Teazel. Without hesitation, the Mastiff hurled itself at the Zygon, wrenching it away from the window and wrestling it to the ground. Teazel's dark muzzle tore at the creature's spongy orange skin, and the Zygon gave a bloodcurdling scream.

'By God, it's Eddie's hound!' Victor declared, a little late in catching on. 'Where did he spring from? Get them, boy!'

Leaving his Zygon victim rasping for breath, with an

ugly wound in the thick blubbery width of its throat, Teazel charged into the field.

Victor turned to Martha and patted her hand. 'Look away and panic not, my dear. Teazel will soon see off these brutes.'

Martha wasn't so sure. Leaving the car, she crossed cautiously to the hole in the hedge; afraid of what she might see but needing to know how bad things were going to get.

To her amazement, the Zygons had gone, apparently scared away. Teazel stood panting in the field, watched only by a few wary cows. Cautiously, Martha turned her attention to the splintered carriage. The door was either locked or jammed shut, and so she peered through the broken window. There was no one inside, just a dark, shadowy shape about the size of a cool box. Was that what the Zygons had been after?

There was further rustling from behind her, on the other side of the road. Turning anxiously, she found Ian trying to wrestle his bike through the foliage. The boy's red cheeks were very nearly the colour of his sweat-soaked hair. As he took in the scene, his eyes widened to the size of saucers.

'You all right, old chap?' asked Victor, putting a hand on his shoulder.

'I was chasing after Teazel,' he panted, staring round in shock. 'He started barking over at Goldspur, and I thought he'd found the intruder Miss Jones saw this morning.'

Victor frowned at her. 'What intruder?'

'That's another story,' Martha told him quickly. 'What happened, Ian?'

'Well, I went with him to the edge of the grounds, and he was barking at the wall, so I helped him scramble up and over…' Ian sank to his knees, exhausted. 'But then Teazel set off ferociously fast, barking loud enough to wake the dead.'

'Going over the wall cuts the distance to reach here,' Victor realised. 'He must've got the scent of these brutes.' He eyed the bodies in the road with revulsion. 'First a giant reptile, now these things. Never seen anything like them.'

'Teazel has,' said Martha. 'He was stung by one. The Doctor calls them Zygons.'

Ian advanced cautiously on the one Teazel had savaged. It held its fists to its bloody chest as if fearing an attack. But then its dark eyes glazed over, and a last breath leaked from its lips.

'A score well-settled, Teazel,' said Victor gravely.

'There's one that won't sting you again,' Martha muttered.

'These Zygons…' Ian looked at Martha. 'Was it they who attacked my father?'

'It's possible.' Martha caught Victor's eye guiltily. 'And that intruder I saw at Goldspur this morning? That was a Zygon too.'

Victor stared at her. 'But why didn't you tell me about

this sooner? For heaven's sake, Miss Jones, the ladies are on their own there!'

'It was Lord Haleston's journal the Zygon was after,' Martha assured him. 'I tried to warn Mrs Lunn an intruder was in the house, but she wouldn't believe me. Would *you* have believed me before you saw all this?'

'Suppose not,' Victor admitted. 'What do they want with us?' Then he saw Ian pluck something from the hand of the newly dead Zygon. 'Don't touch it!' he snapped.

'I— I was only looking,' said Ian standing back up. He held out his discovery – a lump of gristle roughly in the shape of a dagger. 'Could this be a weapon?'

'Could be anything,' said Martha. 'Didn't see him holding it before…'

Suddenly Teazel started barking again, and Martha's stomach twisted. She quickly looked around to see where the next threat was coming from. She couldn't see anything – but moments later, a high-pitched whine filled the air. 'Uh-oh,' said Martha. 'Last time I heard that noise…'

Victor and Ian backed away, as the three dead Zygons in the road glowed with an eerie white light and faded from view.

'Now I've seen it all,' said Victor weakly.

Martha withdrew to a safe distance, beside Teazel. The wind had dropped, and birdsong whistled from the heather and the hedgerows. Only the horse remained now beside the wreck of the carriage, together with dark stains of blood on the road; to anyone else who happened past, there was nothing to suggest this hadn't been a simple, unpleasant accident.

Then Teazel suddenly jumped up and bounded away from them, haring across the moorland.

'Teazel!' Ian bellowed. 'Come back, boy!'

'He's got the scent again,' Victor realised. 'Perhaps he's giving chase to the other two we saw?'

Ian reached for his fallen bicycle. 'I've got to go after him.'

'You can't.' Martha stepped in front of him, blocked his way. The giant dog was already vanishing into the distance. 'It's way too dangerous.' She forced a smile. 'Besides, you saw what he did – he's the Zygon slayer. He'll be all right.'

Ian looked close to tears. He nodded stoically, and turned away.

'I say, the poor horse is still breathing,' Victor declared. 'Perhaps he stands a chance of pulling through.'

'Let's hope so,' said Martha. 'We should telephone for the police to sort things here, as fast as they can.' She sighed. 'And tell Mrs Unswick what's happened to her horse and her friend's carriage.'

'We'll phone from the Lodge then,' said Victor. 'With any luck, Monsieur Romand might be at home, too. I can send him off to Wolvenlath with a message for Henry – Call off the hunt! To hell with the Beast of Westmorland

and medals from the King, we must search Goldspur's grounds and secure the place!'

Martha approved. That'd get everyone out of the Doctor's way for sure.

She allowed Ian to help her up into the back seat of the Opel. He didn't let go of her hand afterwards, and she gave it a reassuring squeeze.

Victor started up the car and drove slowly away through the puddles of blood on the muddy, rutted road.

TWELVE

In the Zygon control room, Analyst Taro watched the black shadows thicken beneath the synchron-response display. 'Three lives lost for nothing,' she hissed, and the glow in the walls darkened as if in sympathy with her mood. 'The greedy fools…'

'I will spread the news among the troops,' said her assistant, Felic. 'Let this violence stand as a stark warning.'

'For how much longer can we survive?' Taro slumped heavily against the monitoring panels. 'Brelarn must end this madness swiftly, or else we must all return to the amber sleep…'

'None know this better than Brelarn,' Felic wheezed loyally. 'Has he not already turned our greatest peril to our best advantage?' The Zygon's eyes were fixed on the image pulsing on the veined scanner screen. It showed a thin, dark-haired man sat alone on a hillside, crouched over an array of electronic parts. 'We shall not have to sleep away the centuries. Our future victories are assured. Whatever plans this Doctor may have, he is playing into the hands of the Zygons.'

From a hillside overlooking Kelmore, the Doctor watched through a pair of opera glasses as labourers struggled and strained to load Sir Albert Morton's construction gear from waterside barn to waiting barge. Before long, no doubt, it would be covering the short distance along the Rochdale canal from here to Eskmouth. From there the roads to Wolvenlath would support a trailer wide enough to complete the distance. What a faff!

The Doctor lowered the glasses. Humans were such determined things, when they thought the cause just enough. He sighed. '*This* just cause will just cause chaos.'

He turned back to the various tiny mechanisms laid out around the trilanic activator beside him. He had the strange – but not altogether unfamiliar – feeling he was being watched. Turning, he found a friendly cow had wandered up behind him.

'Hello!' he called. 'Is my activator bothering you?' He held it up to show her. 'You poor old cows. Bet this used to be a nice, quiet area before all the aliens turned up, didn't it?'

The cow eyed him lazily, then lowered its head to graze.

The Doctor turned back to the sticky Zygon component. 'Haven't got far with connecting a command system to the activator cortex, I'm afraid, Daisy. Organic crystallography, I'm always underestimating it. So I can't tell the Skarasen what to do…' He picked up a small, delicate construction of wire and miniaturised circuitry and squashed it into the side of the fleshy lump. 'Luckily, I'm a lot better with augmented delta waves. And if I can modify these circuits so their delta waves transmit on a *diastellic* wavelength, it should make the Skarasen very, very sleepy.' He buzzed the sonic at his miniature maze of new circuitry. 'And hopefully it should stay nice and dozy till I work out how to send it away and leave us all in peace…'

The cow, unsurprisingly, made no comment, and the Doctor's gaze drifted to the last of the hoists being packed aboard the barge. 'Always assuming I can get to the Skarasen before the hunters, anyway. But with the biggest pile of construction gear in the country stored so handily close by…' He turned back affably to the quietly grazing cow. 'I've heard you should never look a gift-horse in the mouth. But I reckon if Lord Haleston and his chums stopped to look at *this* one, they'd find a gob full of very pointy teeth…'

He tailed off as he realised there was someone else watching him, further up the hillside. A girl with long blonde hair, standing beside a rocky crag that jutted from the grassland.

She was beckoning him.

'Well, well,' the Doctor murmured. 'Molly Melton, the helpful ghost. Only you're no apparition, are you?' He started towards her, slowly. 'Why don't you show me what you *really* are?'

The girl watched him approach with large, sad eyes. Too late, the Doctor felt the coldness of a shadow fall over his back. He whirled round.

But the Zygon was already bringing a rock down against his head.

As Victor pulled up outside Mrs Unswick's lodge, Martha felt Ian grip her hand tighter. Then she saw why.

Nanny Flock was standing outside the front porch. Victor tipped his cap, but the woman ignored him. She was rubbing her hands together, like she was relishing the thought of the coming confrontation.

The moment Victor cut the engine he called over to her. 'What's wrong? Has anything happened at Goldspur?'

'His mother's almost worried herself to death,' the nanny retorted. Her narrow eyes flicked between Ian and Martha. 'I thought I'd find you here, young man,' she said smugly. 'Chasing after *her* again. Your mother refused to believe you could be so irresponsible…'

'Wait here a moment,' Martha told Ian, and she climbed down from the back of the car. 'Whatever your problem is, Miss Flock, we've got bigger ones. All this can wait while we call the police.'

'You've just missed them,' the nanny informed her. 'They were collecting a Frenchman's cinema films. It all sounds very unsavoury.' She glared at Martha. 'In any case, *I'm* the one who should be calling the police. You've led this weak-minded boy astray with your funny foreign ideas!'

'Really, Miss Flock,' said Victor. 'There's been a serious accident barely a mile from here—'

'The phone's out of order, in any case,' the nanny informed him. 'Or I'd use it now to tell the mistress where her little horror's gone. Quite beside herself with worry, she is.'

'How do you know the phone's out of order?' asked Martha.

Nanny Flock bristled. 'I asked the owner, didn't I?'

'Where is she?' Martha realised the front door was ajar and made towards it. 'Mrs Unswick? I've got some bad news about—'

But Nanny Flock barred her path. 'Don't think you're walking away from me again. I've not finished with you yet.'

'Leave her alone,' said Ian fiercely.

'Er… let's all keep our heads, shall we?' said Victor, hurrying to intercede. But Martha had already pushed past the bony woman and opened the door.

She saw the old-fashioned telephone standing on the hall table beside a pile of unopened mail. But the connecting wire had been yanked out of its socket.

'Uh-oh,' said Martha. 'Mrs Unswick?'

Nanny Flock entered the hall after her. 'She said she needed to lie down. Bad for her nerves, I shouldn't wonder, the police coming to call...'

'So she opened the door and gave a total stranger the run of the place?'

'Perhaps she recognises a respectable person when she sees one,' sniped the nanny.

But Martha was already running up the stairs and along the landing to Mrs U's room. 'Hello?' She knocked on the door. 'I'm sorry to disturb you, but...'

No reply. With a shrug, Martha opened the door to the bedroom.

The bed was empty and unmade. There was a strange smell in the air. The same earthy, iron smell she'd caught when...

'Uh-oh.' Swallowing hard, Martha ran out of the room and back down the landing. As she reached the stairs she saw that Victor and Ian were crouched beside the broken telephone. Nanny Flock was closing the front door, eyeing Martha malevolently.

Martha stopped at the bottom of the stairs. 'Victor, Ian, get away from her,' she said, licking her lips. 'She's not what she seems. She's not human!'

'You poisonous creature,' sneered Nanny Flock. 'You should be horse-whipped for saying something like that to an Englishwoman!'

'The Doctor says those creatures can change their

shapes to look like us.' Martha backed slowly away, as Nanny Flock walked purposefully towards her. 'I think she's one of them!'

Her face twisting with rage, Nanny Flock broke into a prim little run – but as she passed the door to the sitting room, a brass blur flashed out and struck her on the forehead with a resounding crash. Poleaxed, she fell to the floor.

Ian stared, open-mouthed, while Victor blinked in disbelief. 'I say…'

Martha stared in amazement as an ill-looking Mrs Unswick shuffled out of the sitting room, wielding a bed-warmer by its long iron handle. 'Not human, you say, dearie? I'll not have any of that in my house!'

'Oh, thank god you're all right,' said Martha, coming to join her on wobbly legs. 'When I couldn't find you upstairs…'

'Oh, don't you worry about me, dear,' said the large woman kindly, putting down the brass bed-warmer. 'Worry about yourself.'

Martha had a fraction of a second to register the cold glint in Mrs Unswick's eyes. By that time, plump fingers were already digging into her arm, pulling her closer. With a half-strangled gasp, Martha found herself caught in a headlock.

'What do you think you're doing, woman?' Victor demanded.

'Let Martha go,' Ian added, his cheeks flushing.

'Stay where you are,' Mrs Unswick ordered. 'Or I'll snap her neck.' She tightened her grip. 'The girl was right to warn you. But that woman on the floor is perfectly human… It's *me* who isn't.'

Martha could hardly swallow as the flabby arm around her throat began to bubble and glow and thicken. A fierce red light shone from alien veins as they forced their way to prominence. The woman's breath was getting shallower, wheezier. The stench of earth and iron flared in Martha's nostrils. She looked down and saw Mrs U's white skirts blacken and shrink away like burning paper. Orange legs showed beneath, ridged with strange bones and muscles.

Ian clutched his stomach, transfixed with horror. 'She's one of those things.'

'We are Zygons,' the creature rasped in its sinister whisper. 'You will not alert others to our presence here. Not now our gambit to take control of this world has begun.'

THIRTEEN

The Doctor's head felt like an old TV set warming up. Sound came first – an eerie, pulsating thrum of energy, rhythmic and monotonous, underpinned by echoing, dripping noises. It was a sound he recognised but couldn't place. He only knew it spelled danger.

He opened his eyes and sight started to return, fuzzy at first. He was lying on something spongy and damp, something that shook softly with the pulse of a giant heartbeat. Then a red-orange glare burned fiercely into his senses.

'The prisoner is awake,' came a hissing whisper.

'The prisoner is an *idiot* to be suckered by the little-girl-distracts-him-while-the-big-Zygon-lamps-him routine,' the Doctor muttered.

Strong hands slipped under his arms and hauled him roughly to his feet. The two Zygons who had hold of him were nothing to look at so he focused instead on the lights that were coming from somewhere inside the fibrous walls, softly growing and fading in intensity. *I'm in their spaceship*, he realised.

The entire control room looked to have been grown rather than made, with gnarled, glutinous control consoles and instrument banks. Vines and creepers lay bundled in place of power cables. Roots and protuberances took the place of levers and switches. The sour tang of blood hung in the air, though the Doctor decided that by rights it should smell like an Italian restaurant; everything seemed covered in bits of pizza and spaghetti, even the big screen on the wall that was showing…

'Martha?' The Doctor shook his head to try and clear it, and stopped when he discovered how much that hurt. But the pain helped him focus. He saw that Martha was standing in the sitting room of the Lodge – they must have a communications link there somewhere. She was staring into the screen imploringly as if she could actually see him, a Zygon's hand pressed against her cheek. 'Martha!' he shouted.

'Doctor?' her voice sounded strained.

'Are you OK?' They both said it at once, both half-smiled.

'Be silent,' hissed the Zygon on the screen, holding its hand harder against her cheek.

'It's Mrs Unswick,' Martha cried. 'She's one of them – *ow*.' She gasped as one of the fingers stroked her temple.

'Get off, that burns!'

'What're you doing to her?' the Doctor shouted, straining towards the screen. But strong arms held him back. 'Let her go! If you harm her…'

A squat, burnt-orange Zygon walked in front of the screen, staring at him from beneath broad, sweaty brows. 'I am Taro,' she hissed, every whispered syllable as sticky as the ship she lived in.

'I don't care what your name is,' the Doctor snapped. 'I want to talk to Martha.'

Taro squeezed a spongy nodule protruding from the console. 'The audio link has been cut.'

'Then find another. You must have loads of those things dotted around the place, keeping in touch—'

'The link was cut deliberately,' Taro said. 'And your friend's throat could quickly follow. Her life is in your hands. Be assured Medri shall sting to kill at the first sign of betrayal.'

The Doctor looked into the creature's dark eyes. 'I'm warning you, now. Just once. Hurting Martha would be a very, very stupid thing to do.' He glanced round the rest of the control room, noting the exits, casually clocking the few controls he understood. 'If Mrs U was really Mrs Z, why not bring me here sooner?'

'It did not serve our interests.' Taro's bloated lips tugged into a smile. 'This ship is submerged beneath Lake Kelmore. You came to our lair of your own free will.'

'Well, apart from having a good gloat, what is it you want from me?' the Doctor demanded. 'I mean, you've ruined my plan, stopped me sending your Skarasen to sleep. You've got the old activator back now.'

Taro duly held it up. 'Tell us how you planned to subdue the Skarasen.'

'Why d'you want to know?' he asked, genuinely interested.

'Tell us, truthfully,' the Zygon insisted. 'Or we shall kill your friend.'

'All right.' The Doctor took a deep breath. 'I thought a burst of energised sound on the right wavelength *might* set the delta-wave generator resonating in harmony with the diastellic signal receptors in the Skarasen's brain. Or in purely sonic terms: *whirrrrr-wheeeee-brbrbrbrbrbrbr-Zzzzzzz.*' He made a snoring noise, then raised his eyebrows. 'Well, you did ask.'

'So the therapy would be non-invasive?'

'You'd know more about invasions than me.' He smiled. 'So! I've answered your questions – here are some of mine. What's going on with little Molly Melton? I mean, why impersonate a child just to have her point people towards your pet monster? And those cranes, the diggers in the barn – the best gear this century can supply for coping with a giant amphibious cyborg… I'm pretty sure *you* ordered them, not Sir Albert Morton – not the *real* Sir Albert, anyway. It's almost like you *wanted* the humans to take on your Skarasen.'

'Be silent, Doctor, or the girl—'

'No!' Angrily, he shook his arms free of the two Zygons and advanced on Taro. 'You won't kill Martha, because you need answers from me. And if you so much as scratch her I'll never tell you a thing.' He slammed his hand down on the weirdly glowing console. '*Never.*'

'Are you so very sure, Doctor?' she whispered. 'We are sole survivors of a stellar calamity. Our ship has crash-landed here. We are alone on this planet. The nearest rescue ship is centuries distant.' She heaved herself towards him. 'We have so little to lose at present. That makes us very dangerous.'

The Doctor saw actual pain in her eyes. He found himself nodding, stepping back down towards the two guards. They watched him beadily, but didn't try to grab hold of him again.

Suddenly a door in one wall slid upwards with a rush of foul air. The Doctor turned as a taller, hulking Zygon entered the control room with the swagger and scars of a bloody-minded general. The guards duly stood to attention.

'Greetings, Commander Brelarn,' said Taro. Though she held herself stiffly, a note of weariness still sounded in her voice. 'I am questioning the Doctor.'

'And he is proving difficult,' Brelarn surmised. His dark eyes bored into the Doctor's. 'You will explain to us the principles of your device.'

'Well, thing is, Mr Brelarn...' He frowned. '*Is it*

mister, or am I underselling you? Brelarn, O.B.E.? *King* Brelarn?'

'I am Warlord of the Zygons.'

'Well, the thing is, your Warlordship,' said the Doctor, 'I haven't been able to lock the wavelength harmonies in phase. And without that, the activator would send out conflicting signals – soothing the Skarasen one moment, stirring it up the next.'

Brelarn turned to the larger of the two Zygon guards. 'Is this likely, Felic?'

Felic slowly inclined his huge domed head. 'Yes, Commander.'

'Then you must solve this problem, Doctor,' Brelarn insisted.

'Why? Surely the last thing you want is for others to be able to control your food supply?'

The Warlord loomed over him menacingly. 'Do not question us.'

'Oh, wait a minute… hang on…' The Doctor looked between Brelarn and Taro. 'You've *lost* control, haven't you? Yes! Yesssss, that's it! Your Skarasen's slipped his leash, and you can't get him back again. Dear, oh dear. To lose one Skarasen is unfortunate, but to lose two… How'd you manage that?'

Taro slumped back against her control bank and stared at him hatefully.

'All that machinery at the manor – it's not a trick, not a trap, is it? It's a helping hand. You want the humans to catch your Skarasen for you.' The Doctor turned to Brelarn. 'You tried to make it as easy as possible for them to find it, even produced a ghostly little waif to point out the likeliest areas.'

'A most successful strategy. Human beings are superstitious creatures. *Sympathetic* creatures.' Brelarn leaned in closer to the Doctor's face. 'Give them a tragic death to avenge and they fight all the harder.'

The Doctor didn't flinch. 'That's what you hoped. But you couldn't be sure, could you? So you've been gathering intelligence. Peeping in diaries, scavenging journals, listening to gossip below stairs…' He frowned. 'All a bit elaborate though, isn't it? A bit pointless, too? Why rely on an "inferior" species to take care of things when surely you could have taken body prints of the hunters and caught the Skarasen yourselves a whole lot faster.' He gave Brelarn a sudden smile. 'I'm missing something, aren't I? What am I missing? Go on, tell me.'

'You must perfect your device,' said Brelarn heavily. 'We must regain control of the Skarasen.'

'The girl is our prisoner,' Taro reminded him. 'And we are holding two others. Unless you have completed the device within the next two hours, we will execute one of them.'

The Doctor looked at her coldly. 'Two hours may not be long enough.'

'We will give you no longer.' Brelarn turned to one

of the other Zygons. 'Take him to the laboratory, Felic. Assist him in his work.'

'Yes, Commander.' Felic took the Doctor by the arm and steered him towards a door that slid upwards into the fleshy ceiling as they approached.

The Doctor turned back round to catch a last look of Martha gazing out of the veined, pulsating screen. But the image was blank. She had gone.

The Zygon marched Martha out of Mrs Unswick's sitting room and up to a closed door. 'Unlock it,' came the inhuman gurgle in her ear.

With a shaky hand, Martha turned the key and twisted the handle. As a reward she was shoved roughly inside, landing flat on her face on the floorboards. The door slammed shut and the key turned with an insolent *shunk*.

Victor and Ian hurried over to help her up. They were in a dingy bedroom, lit feebly by a small oil lamp that sent smoky shadows shaking across the wall with every sputter of its flame.

'What did that thing do to you?' Victor asked, concerned.

'Made a lot of threats, basically.' Martha sat down miserably on the bumpy bed. 'They've taken the Doctor prisoner. I heard his voice…' Ian looked puzzled, and she sighed. 'They had a kind of… magic telephone,' she explained. 'It let me hear him.'

'Magic telephones, conjuring tricks… these brutes are a proper circus attraction.' Victor sat down beside her. 'I shall never in all my days forget the sight of Mrs Unswick turning into that… *thing*.'

'She had me completely taken in.' Martha shuddered. 'She was kind, gave me clothes, even cooked for me… but all the time she was a Zygon. The Doctor was right. They're good at what they do.'

'Wish I'd thought faster,' said Ian. 'When that brute brought you inside, I could have charged the thing and stuck its own filthy knife into it.'

'What?' Martha looked down at the dagger-shaped lump of gristle in his hand. 'You took this from the dead Zygon in the road…'

'Slipped it in my pocket,' he confessed. 'I thought you'd take it off me if you knew I had it…'

Martha studied the thing properly. It looked a bit like a root of ginger, covered with scabs. A drop of green ooze fell from the sharp end onto her finger. It smelt disgusting and she quickly wiped it on the blanket covering the bed.

'I don't think this thing is a weapon,' she said slowly. 'I guess it might be food, or something. Like those tubes of yoghurts kids have in their lunch boxes.' She glanced up at two blank faces. 'Never mind.'

'That dying monster was clutching on to the thing like it was gold,' said Ian.

'Must be a weapon, then,' Victor reasoned, 'or else

why hold on to it while attacking a moving carriage?'

'Maybe it pulled this thing *out* of the carriage,' said Martha slowly. 'Before the crash threw it clear!'

Ian nodded. 'You could be right!'

'But… Zygons stealing from other Zygons?' Martha frowned. 'It doesn't make sense.'

'Maybe not,' said Victor. 'But if that carriage came from here, our friend outside may be very keen to get back its property. Perhaps we can trade this thing for our freedom?'

'And the Doctor's,' said Martha. She crossed to the door and banged on it. 'Oi, Zygon!' she shouted. 'We want to talk. We've got something to show you.'

Silence.

'Maybe if it gets a whiff of the stuff,' Ian suggested, passing her the root. 'You could squeeze a drop under the door…'

'Worth a go,' Martha agreed, jamming the root into the gap between door and floorboards.

The clunk of the key turning a second later was the only warning Martha got. She grabbed the root and scrambled backwards across the floor as the door was kicked open. The Zygon filled the doorway like a hideous demon, hissing like a rattlesnake. Ian and Victor scrambled over the bed to get some distance from it.

'Where is the ration?' the creature snarled, salivating as it lumbered into the darkened room. 'Give it to me.'

Martha spied a crack in the floorboards beside her.

'Stay back!' she warned the Zygon, holding the root over the split. 'Or I'll empty this and you won't get a drop.'

The creature froze, while its shadow raged around the walls in the flickering lamplight. 'Where did you find it?'

'Your… your carriage crashed,' Ian stammered. 'It was attacked by your own people.'

'No. *You* stole it.' The Zygon took a threatening step closer to Martha. 'And I must feed.'

'Got it,' said Martha. 'This stuff's Skarasen milk, isn't it? The Doctor said you all need its lactic fluid to survive.'

'Give me the ration,' the Zygon hissed.

'Why is it being rationed?' Martha rose shakily to her feet. 'Because one of your Skarasens is dead, is that it? And the other one isn't making enough to go round?'

A hideous blocked-drain sound came retching from the Zygon's throat as it broke into a stumbling run, arms reaching out towards Martha.

'Fetch!' she yelled, hurling the root into the far corner of the room.

The Zygon turned clumsily towards the precious ration. Then Victor shoulder-charged the creature, knocking it onto the bed. 'Everybody run!' he shouted.

Martha led the rush for the door. Victor followed first, and then Ian, who slammed the door shut and turned the key, locking the Zygon inside. 'It wasn't bothered with us,' he panted, 'it went after that milk stuff.'

'It acted like it was half-starved,' Martha agreed. 'If the Zygons are that desperate for lactic fluid, it could explain why they attacked the carriage to get their fix of the stuff.' She gasped. 'And if we got our hands on it, we could maybe bargain it for the Doctor's release!'

Someone groaned behind them, as if taking issue. Nanny Flock was recovering. 'I'd managed to forget about her.' Martha crossed quickly to help her up. 'Are you all right?'

'My head hurts,' she mumbled.

Martha examined it. 'You've got a nasty lump but the skin's not broken.'

Nanny Flock pulled crossly away, felt her head for herself. 'What happened?'

A loud banging started up behind the downstairs bedroom door.

'*That* did,' said Ian nervously.

'We'll explain on the way,' said Victor, helping the bony woman to her feet.

'I can manage, thank you,' she informed him primly.

Then the bedroom door was smashed off its hinges. The heavy oak flew across the hall and crashed into Nanny Flock, slamming her to the floor.

Martha winced. 'Not her day, is it?' She grabbed hold of Ian's hand and they backed away as the Zygon strode out into the hall, blocking the way to the front door.

'A quick feed seems to have done it a deal of good,' Victor observed, running to join them.

'Out the back way,' cried Martha, hurrying towards the kitchen. 'Come on!'

With a rasping, gurgling hiss, the Zygon strode after them.

FOURTEEN

In the weirdly lit grotto of the Zygon laboratory, the Doctor had been working on the activator for over an hour. Now and then, Felic would stop to query a procedure or advise on the crystal calibration. But the Zygon was being annoyingly evasive when it came to the real questions on the Doctor's mind.

Even so, there was no harm in trying.

'To be going to all this trouble to gain control over a rogue Skarasen,' he said, 'presumably you've either got lots and lots of them and you can see the problem arising again… Or else you've got very few. Maybe even just one.'

'This matter does not concern you,' hissed Felic.

'It concerns me a lot,' the Doctor snapped, pulling off his glasses. 'I know what just one of your pets can do. And I guess it must concern someone else pretty badly too, or else why would they kill the first Skarasen?'

Felic remained impassive. 'Continue the work.'

'I saw the state of the Skarasen corpse on the lakeshore,' the Doctor persisted. 'Who did it? Why are they after you?'

'*We* destroyed the Skarasen adult,' the Zygon said quietly.

The Doctor stared at him, dumbfounded. 'What?'

'The stellar catastrophe that damaged our ship also affected the brain-computer interfaces of our Skarasens.'

'Supercharged particle emission?'

Felic looked away. 'We did not realise the problem until the two beasts were fully reared beneath the waters here. The brain tissue became inflamed. Our creatures became… deranged. Attempts at diastellic therapy in the adult only aggravated the inflammation. The feedback swamped the control cortex and caused…'

'Yeah.' The Doctor pictured the blackened remains of the Skarasen's steel skull. 'Yeah, I saw what it caused.'

'We tried to recall the juvenile here—'

'Where it ran amok through the village.'

'Its brain is shutting down. This is why it lies stupefied in the lake.' Felic hissed heavily. 'It must be removed and secured long enough to carry out the *correct* therapies. Or else it too will die.'

'Only you don't have the strength to secure it yourselves, now, do you?' The Doctor watched him closely. 'You've tried, you just get mauled. Your little outpost here is dying, just as Taro said. No food, no strength, no protection. And if this Skarasen dies now, so will you. Which is why you've manipulated the humans into capturing it for you.'

'Proceed with the work,' said Felic.

'You know, I thought at first some alien hunter was after you and your Skarasens.' The Doctor gave a mock laugh. 'How wrong was I? There's no one after you, no danger of innocent humans being caught in the crossfire of some alien vendetta. Nah, it's just you Zygons – killing people, stealing away their loved ones and replacing them with your kind...'

'Work!' the Zygon demanded.

The Doctor shook his head. 'You've tricked these people, goaded them into the hunt, let your creation kill and destroy so they have no choice but to go after it. You've pointed out its hiding places to them, because you know that if they leave it alone it'll die, and you with it. Their troubles would be over.' He looked coldly into the black pits of the Zygon's eyes. 'Yeah. Clever con. That's the *real* sting of the Zygons.'

'Humans are an inferior species,' Felic argued calmly. 'But we are few and they are many. If we sought their help openly, they would destroy us.'

'You don't know that,' the Doctor argued.

'Brelarn knows,' said Felic. 'He has proclaimed it. That is enough.' He resumed his dispassionate study of the Doctor's circuits. 'To such as us, the humans are as easy to mimic as they are to provoke. The events we have set in motion will lead not only to our assured survival, but to the triumph of the Zygons over all the Earth.'

With the angry rasping of the Zygon not far behind, Martha pelted through into Mrs U's kitchen with Ian and Victor. She practically hurled herself against the door leading to the garden – then cursed under her breath. It was locked, and the key was nowhere to be seen.

'Is Nanny dead?' asked Ian, white-faced.

'I'm pretty sure she was still breathing,' said Martha, searching desperately for the key on the kitchen table. 'We'll get help and come back for her.'

Victor grabbed a rolling pin and smashed open the window, grinding the wood against the frame to clear the jagged fragments remaining. At the same time, Ian and Martha shoved the table over to block the door.

She caught a glimpse of blood-orange striding through the shadows towards them.

'Come on, urchin!' Victor called, clambering carefully through the window.

Martha helped Ian climb after him and started to follow. She heard the Zygon hiss and the table screech against slate tiles as it was shoved violently aside. Ian and Victor helped her struggle uninjured through the window into the courtyard. The bright sunshine and blue sky made it hard to imagine the nightmare creature inside could be real.

The angry, inhuman bellow suddenly made it a lot easier.

'We've got to get to your car,' gasped Martha, setting off at a run around the side of the house. 'Put some distance between us and that thing.'

'It will hear me trying to start the engine up,' Victor told her, slowing to a halt. 'It could just stroll out and get us.'

Oh, for electric ignition, thought Martha.

'We could get back to Goldspur on foot,' Ian suggested.

'Lot of open countryside between here and there,' said Victor, 'and if the Zygon's got pals abroad…'

'Then we hide,' Martha declared, getting her bearings and setting off again. 'We try to make it think we've run for it. Come on – the stables.'

'Why the stables?' Ian wondered.

'Because they stink,' she said. 'You saw how quickly the Zygon smelt its dinner – maybe all the muck in there will mask the smell of us.'

It didn't take long to reach the now empty stables. Ian and Victor followed Martha inside, right to the back. Their footsteps through the wet straw sounded like pistol cracks in her ears, but she couldn't hear the Zygon. Trying not to imagine what she must be stepping in, and trying harder not to gag at the stench, she settled down in the thickest shadows of the stall, Ian and Victor crouching beside her. Flies buzzed around them.

'It smells like something crawled in here and died,' hissed Ian, speaking through his shirtsleeve.

Martha nodded. There was something hard beneath the straw. Something they could use to defend themselves? She felt with her fingers.

And touched someone else's.

For a moment, Martha didn't dare look down. The fingers were hard and cold. She felt a lacy cuff on a wrist, snatched her fingers away. Saw a silver bracelet with a charm in the shape of a 'C'.

'What is it?' Victor whispered.

Martha moved some of the damp straw away to reveal a woman's arm, a white apron-string loose at the shoulder.

'*Always sticking her beak into other people's business, was Clara,*' Mrs Unswick had said, smiling in her sitting room.

'Oh my god…' Martha said quietly. Steeling herself, she looked down and saw the gleam of a knife protruding through the straw, wedged squarely in the maid's back.

'*She made off in the night with some of my best silver!*'

'Martha?' Victor asked again.

'Nothing,' said Martha, mindful of Ian beside her. 'I just—'

'Shh!' Ian whispered.

Over the thrum of her heart, Martha could hear padding footsteps outside. The Zygon had stolen Mrs Unswick's body and killed Clara, presumably because she'd seen too much. The clothes Martha had found in the wardrobe, they hadn't been left for her at all – only left behind. Now, for certain, she knew the creature would not hesitate to butcher them in cold blood.

She held her breath, covered her mouth and nose with the sleeve of her cardigan, shuddered as she realised it belonged to this corpse. She felt Ian press his face against her shoulder, heard the ragged breathing of the thing outside, and wondered if their scent would carry over the wet straw, horsehair and filth. And if so, would it put the human stench down to poor Clara, or would it know that they…

No. At last, the Zygon moved away, its sticky footsteps slapping down in a hurry over the cobbles.

'All right,' Victor whispered. 'We'll stay here for a few minutes, check the coast is clear, get the motor started, check on Miss Flock and push off sharpish.'

'Agreed,' said Martha shakily. Ian and Victor both got up, but she lingered for a moment longer to place her hand on the dead girl's shoulder. *I'm wearing your clothes,* she thought. *But I'm not going to end up in your shoes. Me and the Doctor, we'll get those things that killed you, and…*

Oh, Doctor, where the hell are you?

'Come on,' Ian whispered.

Leaving Clara behind in the fetid straw and darkness, Martha crept away after him.

The harsh swipe of a door sliding upwards made both

Felic and the Doctor turn. A familiar golden-haired child stood swaying in the mouth of the Zygon laboratory.

'Well, well, here's our friendly ghost.' The Doctor watched as the little girl shuffled inside the lab, blank-faced – and with an identical twin following just behind her. 'Hang on, who's that, then? The *real* Molly Melton?'

But that theory was blown out of the water as Mollies three and four came into the lab. Then the first began to glow red, her childish features began to twist and distort…

Suddenly the Doctor was looking at a small, underdeveloped creature with pale, maggoty skin, stumpy limbs and dark shining eyes. Nodules stuck out from the head and chest like wet mouths in the flesh. And now the other three Mollies were changing too, warping through the crimson haze into near-identical creatures.

'Children,' breathed the Doctor. 'It's your *children* you're using.' One of the pale figures sank to its knees, and he stooped to examine it. But Felic pulled him back with a warning rattle.

Then Brelarn strode into the laboratory, holding another of the pale, slimy children in his arms. 'The synchron response in these hatchlings is failing,' he announced. 'They must return to the amber.'

'So this is how Molly Melton makes her spooky visitations to hunters all over the Lakes,' said the Doctor, a sneer in his voice. 'Child labour. You really *are* desperate, aren't you, Brelarn?'

'In war, all must play their part,' came the harsh whisper. Brelarn set down the twitching figure in his arms on the floor and marched over to the Doctor. 'The hatchlings are not yet mature. They are mute, with only limited intelligence, and scant feeling for strategy. But they cover the ground swiftly, and body-print compatibility is—'

'They're kids!' the Doctor shouted. 'Look at them! Half-starved and worked to the point of exhaustion.'

Brelarn gripped the Doctor's cheeks hard between fingers and thumb. 'They are *my* hatchlings,' he whispered. 'They are proud to serve me.'

'Well, you did say they had limited intelligence.' The Doctor felt sharp, prickling points pressing at his skin, but he was too angry to let things go. 'If your own hatchlings are starving, how bad must your soldiers have it? Who are they impersonating in the human world? Can't be anyone too taxing – no wonder "Mrs Unswick" had to have a lie down today, no wonder the trooper I met on the moor this morning was so feeble.' He flashed a small, squashed but defiant smile. 'And no wonder you need me so badly to fix the situation for you.'

With a low growl, Brelarn pushed the Doctor to the floor. Then he turned to Felic. 'Prepare the hatchlings for the amber.'

Felic was already scraping a fine, dark powder from the sides of an orifice in the glowing wall. 'Yes, Brelarn.'

The Warlord left the room, and the door whooshed down behind him.

'What *is* the amber, Felic?' the Doctor asked, jumping back up to his feet. 'Some sort of suspended animation?'

The Zygon grunted. 'This powder will hold them stable in the long sleep until nourishment can be given.' He lifted one of the hatchlings and placed it on a kind of sticky cradle of red sponge growing out of the wall. But the effort seemed to leave him exhausted, and he had to wait a few moments before turning to scoop up the next. 'Return to the work,' he wheezed. 'Your friend will die if you delay.'

'Who's delaying?' The Doctor picked up the third infant from the ground and passed it to Felic with a winning smile. 'I think this little lash-up is about ready to try.' He pulled a face. 'Of course, if the juvenile Skarasen's brain is impaired, we may still have some problems maintaining control. That's not a problem in the device, it's a problem in your Skarasen's head – so if anything goes wrong, you can't hurt my friend, got it?'

'You are a prisoner.' Felic placed the last of the infants in a cradle and wiped black powder about its lips. 'You cannot dictate terms.'

'Oh? That's a pity.' The smile crept back onto his face as he waggled the device and his sonic screwdriver in front of Felic. 'Because since these are my toys and no one can work them better than me, I reckon that makes *me* best qualified to put the Skarasen under the 'fluence so you can work those cyborg synapses.'

Felic gave a warning rattle.

'Look, you can threaten my friends, hold me at sting-point, whatever. I'll go along with it – because I want this Skarasen back under control. That way you can feed up, go back into hiding and stay out of trouble till the rescue ships come in a few centuries' time, and me and Martha can push off and leave you to it. No hard feelings, we'll let bygones be Zygons…' The Doctor winked. 'Whaddya say?'

The door hissed upwards, and Brelarn stalked back inside. 'Very well, Doctor,' he rumbled. 'You *shall* gain control of the Skarasen for us.'

'Good one, big fella,' said the Doctor. 'You know it makes sense.'

Brelarn watched him and smiled…

FIFTEEN

Back on the bumpy, rutted lanes with the petrol-guzzling roar of the motor car in her ears, Martha didn't feel much safer. The Zygon had not come running at the first turn of the crank handle. It hadn't even showed as she, Ian and Victor screeched away in a hail of gravel. She almost wished it had. It would make her feel better for not staying to search for Miss Flock. The nanny's body had disappeared from the hall. Ian reckoned she'd made her own break for it, and Martha hoped that was true.

'We made it!' whooped Victor as they thundered along the road to Goldspur. But Martha couldn't feel too elated. Not while the Doctor was still a Zygon prisoner.

It's OK, she told herself, trying to keep the prickle of tears at bay. *They haven't got you to use against him now. He'll sort them out… Course he will.*

Trying to stay positive, she let her thoughts drift to

Mrs Unswick. She supposed certain things made sense now. Like the way she and the Doctor had disturbed Mrs U in her private movie screening; never mind an inquisitive woman fascinated by new technology, she must have been scouring it to be sure there was nothing in Romand's film that would give the Zygons away to the police when they came to collect it. Or maybe she'd wanted to watch the different hunting parties at work, to study their techniques, their position, their mood. Intelligence gathering.

Martha shuddered. These things were already quite intelligent enough.

'Hold on,' said Victor, peering into the wing mirror. 'I recognise that Rover 20…'

She turned round and started waving excitedly. 'It's Claude!'

Victor stopped the car and motioned Romand to pull up alongside.

The Frenchman did so. 'My friends,' he called, 'is all well?'

'Not remotely,' said Victor. 'Did you happen to come along the main Kelmore road?'

Romand frowned. 'Yes. I have been driving round the area, filming other hunters at work. I was just heading back to Wolvenlath. Why, what has happened?'

'You didn't see the crashed carriage on one of the bends?' asked Martha. 'An injured horse?'

'There was nothing,' he told her.

Ian sighed. 'I suppose if those Zygon things were desperate enough to attack that carriage while it was still moving, a sitting target would be irresistible.'

Martha nodded and glanced round nervously. 'Speaking of sitting targets…'

'You're right, we shouldn't tarry,' said Victor. 'Monsieur Romand, would you mind taking Miss Jones and Ian on to Wolvenlath with you? I must away back to Goldspur.'

'I'm staying with you,' Ian insisted. 'I have to know Mother and Father are safe.'

'Very well, urchin,' Victor grumbled.

'Safe?' Romand frowned. 'What has happened?'

'It's a long story,' said Martha. 'But some intruders have been sighted, both at Goldspur and at the Lodge. We need to go to Lord Haleston for help.'

'Yes, rally the hunting party,' said Victor. 'Haleston knows the chief inspector for these parts. We'll band up with the police, secure Goldspur all together, have a proper hunt round for Miss Flock at the Lodge, then see if we can't find the Doctor at Kelmore.'

If Martha hadn't been so exhausted she might have attempted a hysterical laugh. 'You make it all sound so straightforward.'

'I hope we find Teazel, too,' said Ian solemnly, surveying the empty fields around them. 'Oh, Teazel, boy, where are you?'

'Come on, old chap,' said Victor, forcing jolliness into

his tone. 'I'm sure Teazel will soon return a conquering hero. Why, the King will probably want to give *him* a medal when he arrives…'

Romand's eyes widened. 'The King?' Martha half-smiled to see him look back automatically for his battered movie camera. 'He is coming here?'

Ian nodded. 'He'll be arriving at Stormsby Castle tomorrow!'

'His Highness is a keen hunter,' Victor explained. 'Quite naturally he wants to see the downed beast at the lakeside with his own eyes, and get the proper lecture from his old pal Lord Haleston.'

'His Majesty will have soldiers with him, won't he?' Ian reflected. 'Perhaps we should ask them for help.'

'Whoa, urchin, whoa,' said Victor. 'One step at a time.'

'Speaking of time,' Martha said, with a pointed look at Romand.

He seemed away in a world of his own. 'But this is wonderful! Imagine if I could *film* the King's examination of the Beast with Lord Haleston. A truly historical moment, no?'

'You can ask Haleston when we get to Wolvenlath,' said Martha firmly, getting out of Victor's car and climbing in beside Romand. 'Now, step on it.'

As Victor and Ian rumbled away and Romand followed on, Martha rubbed her aching back. She decided she would never complain about travel by TARDIS again.

If she ever got the chance.

At last the Rover juddered past a large, granite millstone marked Wolvenlath, by the side of the rucked-up road. The path ahead forked, one way into forest and the other over a hill, and Romand stopped while considering which way to take.

But when the car kept vibrating beneath them, Martha knew straight away that something big was happening.

Correction. Something big was coming right at them.

Martha yelled in horror as the Skarasen came crashing out of the forest close beside them, rending and upending trees with its claws. Its huge eyes gleamed like black ice as it tossed its head from side to side, like a wrecking ball swinging from the thick, snaking neck. Then it seemed to notice the car, and stopped suddenly in its tracks.

Martha threw herself from the car and scrambled for the cover of the roadside bushes. 'Get out!' she yelled to Romand.

But Romand seemed mesmerised by the sight of the Skarasen. The monster opened its jaws and screeched at ear-splitting volume, took another step forwards, splintered a giant oak with a razor-sharp lash of its tail. Its drooling jaws stretched open as it stared down at the motor car.

'Romand!' Martha yelled again.

But then, past the uncertain growl of the engine and the gravel-gargling roar of the Skarasen, Martha heard a voice shouting, *soaring* over the din.

'No, Haleston! I told you, no guns. I can get the Beast back under control…'

She couldn't believe it. 'Doctor?'

Suddenly, the Skarasen's fury seemed to subside. It stopped its thrashing, actually held still, angling its head to one side like it was listening to something…

'See? No need for panic. Leave this to the expert.'

Doubting her senses and abandoning her cover, Martha ran towards the sound of the Doctor's voice, grinning her head off. 'Doctor!'

'Martha!' He saw her coming and stared, astounded. 'You escaped! You're all right!'

She ran to him all the faster. 'Just! How about you?'

'Sort of complicated…' He pointed up at the swaying Skarasen, like a tourist posing with one of the dinosaurs at Crystal Palace. 'Got the trilanic activator working.'

She reached him at last and threw her arms around his neck. 'How the hell did you get away, anyway? I only had one Zygon to get rid of, you must've had a whole ship full…'

Suddenly, he went rigid in her arms and shouted past her: 'Haleston, I meant it – *no*. Start blasting at the Skarasen and you'll bring it out of its trance!'

Martha sprung away to find Lord Haleston had stumbled out of the forest, his clothes caked in dirt, aiming his shotgun at the Skarasen's head while glaring at the Doctor. 'May I remind you, sir, that the beast has already emerged once from your spell, and almost did for the lot of us.'

The Doctor ignored him. And Martha could see now that other hunters were emerging, red-faced and wild-eyed, their clothes covered in mud and bloodstains. She supposed that after a long day spent itching to blast holes in this thing, they were unhappy to be thwarted by this strange, skinny interloper, crashing their party.

'How *did* you get away?' Martha repeated.

The Doctor lowered his voice. 'I was let out. Temporarily.' He held up the fleshy lump with its metal implants and his voice dropped even further. 'This is my gadget, so no one can work it better than me – and the Zygons know that. They're too desperate to take chances.' He gave her a funny look. 'They're meant to be holding you hostage to make sure I don't try anything.'

'Then it's lucky I'm just too good, isn't it?' She smiled. 'Well, me and Victor and Ian are, anyway. The Zygon guard was weak, starving, it's been on rations…' Her face clouded. 'Didn't stop it killing Clara, though.'

The Doctor frowned. 'What, there was another human locked up with you?'

'Hello?' Martha tugged at her clothes. 'Maid at the Lodge who disappeared in the night?'

The Skarasen emitted a low, keening wail that almost made it sound like it was sorry. Its coal-black hide heaved and swelled with deep, shuddering breaths. Talk about sitting on a powder keg – or standing underneath one…

'Doctor,' Haleston broke out impatiently, 'if you're set on playing the pied piper for this thing all the way to Templewell, could you perhaps exercise a little urgency?'

'All right, hang on,' said the Doctor tetchily, peering at his device. 'I'll just up the wave frequency a couple of remars…'

'Remars?' Martha wondered.

He nodded. 'Zygon term.'

'And really, Miss Jones,' Haleston went on. 'I feel it might be best if you could postpone your conversation and get to a place of safety with all haste.'

'No, she's staying with me,' said the Doctor. He turned to her, his voice low again: 'If they're watching me, then they'll know you've escaped. They'll come for you.'

'We're surrounded by armed men,' Martha reasoned. 'That should keep them away. Speaking of which, Victor wanted me to bring everyone back to Goldspur – I told him about that Zygon I saw this morning, and he's afraid there may be others about.'

The Doctor snorted. 'The Zygons are highly intelligent beings trying not to starve to death. Why would they want to go after a few women and an invalid?' He shook his head. 'Anyway, don't mention orange blobby monsters to old Haleston now.' He pointed discreetly up at the Skarasen. 'I need everyone focused. We've got to get this thing secured as soon as possible.'

'Why Templewell, anyway?' Martha asked.

'Easier to secure a single site,' said Haleston, overhearing her as he marched over. 'My equipment's already set up, the lakeside's nicely sheltered from prying eyes... plus, it's closer to the canal than here. The cranes, the chains, the hoists and diggers, they're being unloaded in Templewell now.' He glanced over to where Romand was sat in his car fiddling with his camera, and his craggy features frowned in thought. 'I say, Miss Jones, do you think we could hijack that French newshound's autocar? It could help us lead the Beast to Templewell all the faster, while the men and the hounds can follow on in the carriages.'

And we'll all get back to Goldspur sooner, thought Martha. *Just in case Ian and Victor do run into trouble.*

'I'll go and ask Monsieur Romand,' she offered. She jogged back to the car and gave him a brief rundown of the situation.

'So the Doctor is well after all, yes?' Romand murmured, still staring up in wonder at the docile Skarasen. 'I am glad. And I am delighted to be of service to Lord Haleston...' A crafty smile spread over his face. 'If, in return, my camera and I might be given privileged access to the sensational stories that will soon be unfolding...'

Martha smiled too. 'You journalists, you're just so giving.'

Romand cupped both hands around his mouth and shouted: 'My car and my services are at your disposal, your grace.'

Lord Haleston nodded with satisfaction and hurried over, the Doctor just behind him. 'Much obliged, Monsieur.'

He climbed in beside Romand, and the Doctor and Martha rode in the back. The Doctor's face was lined with concentration as he studied his little gadget, giving the sonic screwdriver cautious little squeezes now and then.

The Skarasen raised one enormous clawed foot and took a sleepwalking step after them. The hunters reacted busily, shouting and backing away, and Romand, with some difficulty, started to turn the car around over the long grass and deep ruts in the road. Martha wondered if Victor and Ian were all right, if the Zygons had seen her here… and if, even now, they were plotting to get her back.

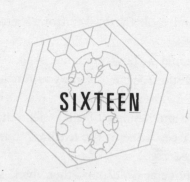

SIXTEEN

'So far, so good,' muttered Ian as Victor's battered motor car trundled along Goldspur's winding drive. The most threatening animal life he had spied so far were a couple of cows who had strayed onto Haleston's land from a neighbouring field; but since all they threatened were the immaculate lawns, Ian decided it was an intrusion they could afford to ignore for now.

'Hello, what's this?' said Victor as they pulled up outside the grand old house. A horse and carriage was just leaving; the driver touched his cap absently as he rode past. Ian saw a woman had been dropped off outside the house.

'Mother!' he cried. She was dressed simply but elegantly as usual in a blue dress. He threw his arms around her so hard that he knocked her shopping basket from her grip. Victor retrieved it for her.

'Ian! Goodness, what a display!' She gently pushed

him away and took the basket from Victor without comment.

Now Ian could see how tired she looked. 'Where have you been, Mother? Were... were you out looking for me?'

'I had to go into Kendall to send a telegram.' Irritation crossed her face. 'It seems the telegraph lines here are out of service.'

'No telephone at Goldspur either, then,' said Victor gravely.

'I had hoped I might spy you along the way, Ian.' She pursed her lips. 'You know, I'm quite furious with you, darling. I've been so worried for you, and so has Nanny Flock. You should feel very guilty, she's gone out searching for you, trying to put my mind at rest.'

Ian's mouth went dry. He looked to Victor to speak for him.

'Yes, well... It's rather my fault, I'm afraid, Cynthia. I saw young Ian as I was driving back from Kelmore and offered him a ride. We did bump into Miss Flock, actually...' Victor cleared his throat. 'Thing is, old girl... well. Nothing unusual has happened here in our absence, has it?'

'Unusual?' She looked puzzled. 'Not remotely. Not since that awful Jones woman came to call this morning.'

'Has the study window been boarded up?' Ian asked urgently.

His mother nodded. 'Chivvers had to get somebody in. He said he'd forward the bill to Mrs Unswick.'

'I shouldn't if I were him,' muttered Victor. 'How about Lady Haleston, is she well?'

'Lady Haleston and the others were in the drawing room when I left them, playing bridge…' She held a hand to her head. 'Which, I trust you'll agree, is not remotely unusual.'

Victor looked at her, concerned. 'Are you feeling all right, Cynthia?'

'Forgive me…' She forced a smile. 'My nerves are bad today.'

'Is Eddie feeling better?'

'He's been sleeping a good deal. I should look in on him now.' She smiled wanly and went to the door, which had been left open. 'Do please excuse me.'

'Well, it seems our fears were unfounded,' said Victor, looking relieved. 'Even so, let's have a quick scout about the grounds, eh?'

'I'm with you,' Ian agreed. 'Perhaps we'll spy Teazel.'

'I'm sure he's making his own way back even now,' said Victor, clapping a hand on Ian's shoulder. 'Come along, then. Off we march!'

Lord Haleston felt his heart kick at his ribs as he watched the giant Beast stamp after them through the deserted countryside. It didn't feel right, relying on the invention of this mercurial Doctor in place of his own mettle. But what alternative was there? This creature was not only a dire threat to human society; it was the zoological find of the century. For both these reasons, it had to be subdued.

He had spent a discouraging day overseeing the firing of shot and the dropping of boulders into the waters of the lake. The beast had simply refused to show itself. Then the Doctor had ridden up on a dark horse, and within minutes of producing his infernally unlikely contraption, had summoned the second Beast of Westmorland to appear before them. It seemed he could even command the thing.

A lot of the men had complained there was no sport in that. But when the Beast had slipped out of the 'fluence and almost killed a man with a casual claw – and since the resultant volley of gunfire had left not the slightest scratch on its hide – they were less vocal in their protests when the Doctor managed to regain control. And once the Beast had started to follow the impertinent fellow into the forest like a lovelorn maid, Haleston had wasted no time sending word to the steam barge with the construction tools aboard to divert to Templewell…

'The sooner this thing is chained up and fully secured, the better,' Haleston commented aloud.

'It's a sick animal,' said the Doctor from the back of the car. 'It needs medical help.'

'Help? That brute?' Haleston shook his head, marvelling at its size, at its sheer power.

'It is a truly remarkable specimen, no?' Romand chimed in. 'Worthy of preserving on film for all time...'

Haleston considered. 'You may have something there.'

'Can't you speed up a little?' Martha enquired, as the gradient of the road steepened. 'That thing will be able to keep up with us.'

Haleston was about to agree gladly when the Doctor jumped in. 'No, keep at this speed.' He held up his curious device. 'The vibration of the engine is already threatening to interfere with the the diastellic signal.' He glared at Haleston: 'If you want to stay alive – we keep at this speed.'

Something in his tone made Martha shiver, and Lord Haleston went very quiet too. Then she remembered that the Doctor had come up against angry Skarasens before. She could imagine it wasn't an experience he was keen to repeat.

They reached the crest of the hill. Behind the Beast, following at a safe distance, Haleston could see the convoy of carriages trailing in single file along the road. It was a reassuring sight.

'Lord Haleston, I wish to make a small confession,' Romand announced. 'Though I am happy to help you in this matter, my services are not given from purely noble motives.'

'Oh?'

Romand smiled. 'I understand from Mr Meredith that

His Royal Majesty is soon to arrive in the area, and that he is interested in this Beast, yes?'

Haleston frowned. 'You understand correctly. What of it?'

'I was wondering if I might be allowed to capture the King's first inspection of this remarkable animal with my camera?' Romand shrugged. 'Think of the newsreels – the most sensational royal visit in all history!'

Lord Haleston frowned. 'I am not sure the world is ready to view such a scene,' he said. 'We may need to hush all this up, you know.' He turned to look again at the remarkable creature stomping slowly after them, and felt a small rush of pride. Such a gargantuan beast – and yet he had overseen its capture. His work as a naturalist had never won him much attention up till now. But this…

He eyed Romand thoughtfully. 'Tell me, sir. While this matter may not yet be fit for the public… might you accept a private commission?'

'Please explain, your grace?'

'The King will be holding a ceremonial dinner at Stormsby Castle, where he will award medals to certain men of service in this brave endeavour.' Lord Haleston cleared his throat. 'I thought perhaps it would be meet to immortalise the occasion in moving pictures for future generations…'

'Yes, for future generations,' said Martha lightly. 'Of course.'

'Let's just hope I can keep the Skarasen under control,' said the Doctor. 'Or else the only small, private ceremonies you'll be attending are your own funerals.'

Ian and Victor had spent a fruitless hour searching the grounds for Zygons. The only remotely sinister sighting was that the gate to the paddock was open and there were no horses in the field.

'Can't imagine a Zygon on horseback,' Victor reflected as they walked back round to the front of the house.

'Perhaps the horses were taken so we couldn't ride them to escape an attack,' worried Ian.

'In that case, perhaps we should be grateful they've spared us the sight of Mrs Chisholm galloping away bareback,' joked Victor, jogging up the steps to the door and ringing the bell.

Ian noticed a piece of paper lying at the foot of the steps and bent to retrieve it. 'Hey, Victor.'

'What do you have there?'

'Looks to be a telegram, sent by Lord Haleston.' His gaze flicked over the neatly typed message. 'Confidential. To the Prime Minister!'

'Give it here,' said Victor. He plucked the paper from Ian's fingers and read aloud. 'Most urgent I see you… Nature and motives of Beast must be discussed… Delicate matter…'

'He's invited half the Cabinet here!' blurted Ian.

'Keep mum, my young buck. This wasn't meant

for your eyes,' Victor cautioned him. 'What I don't understand is, what's it doing out here? It's dated today, but Lord Haleston's been leading the troops at Wolvenlath and your mother said the telegraph lines weren't working. So how did he send such a message?'

Ian frowned. 'Perhaps… no, that doesn't make sense.'

'What?'

'I was just supposing…' He looked at Victor. 'Perhaps it fell from Mother's basket.'

As he spoke he heard the door creak. As if summoned by his very mention, his mother now stood watching them. She looked startled and pale.

'Cynthia?' Victor looked puzzled. 'Where's Chivvers?'

'Indisposed, I imagine. I was just passing the door, when…' She looked at the floor. 'Victor, would you mind awfully seeing where Chivvers has got to?'

'No, of course not,' Victor muttered, stuffing the note in his pocket and marching away.

Ian felt his stomach pinch. 'Is Father all right?'

'He's been asking after you,' she said, and offered him a brave smile. 'Would you like to see him?'

Feeling suddenly very grown up, Ian nodded and followed her inside. She ushered him up the stairs. The butterflies in his belly were tickling every nerve as he walked along the landing to his father's door.

'Father?' he murmured. No reply. He looked to his mother, who wore a tight smile and nodded her head encouragingly.

Inside the bedroom, the deep red richness of the sunset was blocked by velvet drapes. It was gloomy and oppressively hot. His father was hunched up in the four-poster bed.

'How are you feeling, sir?' Ian ventured.

The figure in the bed shifted.

'I'm afraid he's taken a turn for the worse, Ian,' said his mother softly.

Suddenly the figure sat up. Ian felt the hairs on his neck prickle and rise, felt his heart stand still as he looked into the narrowed eyes of a Zygon.

'Mother, get back!' he gasped, stumbling backwards.

A low groaning sound rattled in the back of his mother's throat. He turned to find her engulfed in a haze of red light, blocking the door, her pretty face shrinking and puckering, her head ballooning, the skin spiking with thick, fleshy growths.

Ian screamed, though as the Zygon hiding in his mother reached out for him he knew it was already far, far too late.

Victor cautiously opened the door to Lord Haleston's study. Since Chivvers was absent from his quarters, he thought the man might be assessing repairs to the broken window.

But Chivvers was lying dead on the carpet, his face hideously marked and swollen.

'Oh my God,' Victor murmured. He made a half-hearted attempt to close the man's staring eyes, but the lids wouldn't budge. He rose quickly. *Whatever did this*, he thought, *it could still be around…*

Then he heard the terrified scream.

'Ian?' He dashed back out into the corridor, ready to run to the lad's aid – when a loud bark sounded behind him.

He turned in surprise and alarm. 'Teazel! The noble Teazel, thank heavens!' The English Mastiff's huge dark muzzle was flecked with white froth, and he was panting fit to burst – he must have been running for miles. 'Alas, no rest yet,' Victor muttered, sprinting down the corridor. 'Your young master needs us. Come on, boy.'

The large dog bounded after him – and then locked his fearsome jaws around Victor's leg.

With a gasp, Victor stumbled and fell, twisting round so he fell on his back in the middle of the passage. 'What the deuce…?' Teazel's heavy paws pressed down on his chest, his teeth were bared, eyes narrowed and fierce.

Then suddenly, a halo of light surrounded the Mastiff. Victor whimpered as the dog's limbs began to stretch and warp. The animal's body glowed orange-red as the fawn fur burned away. Alien flesh crazed with veins and nodules thickened round the bones. The canine jaws retracted even as the face fattened and spread.

'No,' croaked Victor, struggling even to draw breath with the weight of the creature on his chest. 'You… you can't be one of them.'

'I am Brelarn, human,' the monster hissed, its breath rank in Victor's nostrils as the light faded from his form. 'Warlord of the Zygons.'

'Then… Teazel…?'

'The animal was captured and brought back to our ship for service. The body of such a beast is most practical, is it not?' Brelarn snorted. 'Swift and powerful, it gains me access to the heart of human affairs and leaves me free to roam outside as I choose.'

'But…' Victor stared helplessly into the alien eyes. 'I saw you attack those Zygons… *Kill* them…'

Brelarn hissed. 'They were committing an act of mutiny. The penalty is death; the sentence mine to impose as I choose.' The Zygon pressed his fingers to Victor's throat and gave a gloating chuckle. 'You humans will beg for the same penalty, once I have enslaved your miserable world.'

Victor couldn't breathe. His skin burned beneath the creature's touch. He heard Ian scream again but the corridor was spinning now, blackness was brushing away his thoughts.

He heard the inhuman, gurgling voice of Brelarn close in his ear: 'Soon, all humanity will be yoked to the will of the Zygons.'

The Skarasen had tripped sleepily through the countryside, oblivious to the convoy of horse and carriages trailing it to Templewell, or the sheep and cattle watching curiously from fields by the roadside. For Martha, the long minutes had passed tensely.

As they neared the site, Lord Haleston bellowed at people to make way, to prepare the machinery.

'Don't start any engines,' the Doctor warned them. 'Not till I've put this thing deep, deep under.' He started to explain how, since the Skarasen had now reached its destination, he could start to close down those areas of its brain that controlled movement and response to stimulus. But Martha was too busy imagining what the creature could do if he messed up to worry much about the technical explanation.

If the Skarasen cared about the presence of its dead fellow, or even noticed, it showed no outward sign. It simply lay obediently down beside it, hindquarters sinking down into the muddy lakeshore.

Martha stared down at it now from a hillock within the cordoned-off area. The Skarasen looked for all the world like a huge dog curled up in sleep, heedless of the hectic rush and din all about it as hunters, naturalists and police swarmed over the site. It did not stir as men hurled steel netting over its head, as a crane haltingly lowered huge boulders onto either side of the metal web to secure it. The dark sheets of its eyelids didn't twitch as the ditch-digger gouged a deep pit out of the shore. More men toiled close by, looping lengths of heavy chain about the Skarasen's talons and fitting them to a hoist. Soon that hoist would lower one of the monster's massive paws into the pit, where it would be secured with more chains and buried beneath tons of earth.

Martha found herself feeling almost sorry for the thing.

The Doctor had been bossing people around, telling them how best to secure the Skarasen, pointing out potential pitfalls, probably annoying the hell out of most of the hunting party. He really seemed an expert. Now he came and slumped down beside her. His characteristic manic energy seemed finally to have deserted him.

'That should slow the Skarasen down for a couple of seconds if things go wrong during the brainwave therapy,' he said moodily.

'So you've done what the Zygons wanted,' said Martha. 'Can't you quickly make the Skarasen push off to the Arctic or wherever before they come to get you?'

'It's not that easy.'

'Well, let's make a quick getaway back to Goldspur – surely we can warn everyone about the Zygons now?'

'We should plan our next moves, definitely.' The Doctor stood up. 'Away from prying eyes. Come on.'

'Oh yeah?' She raised her eyebrows. 'Clandestine rendezvous, is it?'

'Lord Haleston has had a hut built for his personal use.'

'You been spying on him?'

'Of course.'

He led the way up a rocky slope and Martha saw it – a small wooden shack built into a small copse, some way off from the bustle of the lakeshore.

Once inside, Martha found it smelt of pipe smoke. There was a desk and a chair and a cluttered bookshelf. A *thinking space*, she decided.

'That's better,' said the Doctor, closing the door behind her. 'Bit of privacy, just what I was after.' He grinned. 'Because, you see… I can't sting you in this form.'

'What?' Martha felt a shudder go through her. 'That's not funny.'

Still smiling, the Doctor took a step towards her…

SEVENTEEN

Martha tried to push past the Doctor to get to the door, but his hands caught hold of her wrists. 'Get off me,' she hissed, pulling free, backing away. But she soon came up against the desk. There was nowhere to hide or run.

'No wonder you didn't want me telling anyone about Zygons,' said Martha, her cheeks feeling hot.

'You were very obliging,' he said, still smiling. 'It wouldn't be very convenient, a lot of men with guns running round Goldspur.'

'Where's the real Doctor?' she demanded

The doppelganger shook his head. 'You'll never see him again.'

'I should have guessed when you didn't know who Clara was,' she said. 'You may have got the moves and mannerisms, but the real Doctor would never have forgotten her.'

'Oh, I figured it out in the end,' the fake assured her. 'She was the young girl who lived at the house we converted into a supply station, right?'

'So that carriage that crashed *was* the same one I saw at the Lodge – or should I say, the Zygon drop-in centre?'

'That is correct.' He took a step towards her. 'A forward base.'

'And your Mrs Unswick was running the local milk round, right? Sending out the rations to your poor starving spies in the countryside.' As she spoke, Martha was feeling behind her on the desk for any kind of weapon. *Must keep him talking.* 'So – what made you kill Clara? Saw you as you really are, did she?'

The Doctor's smile looked more of a grimace now she knew what lay behind it. 'Like this, you mean?'

Martha suddenly had that familiar nightmare feeling – when you know something awful is going to take place but you can't stop it happening. As she watched, the Doctor's bony features began to warp, to scrunch up into the centre of a huge, blood-red head. He shrank in height but swelled in size, piling on pounds of red-orange flesh.

'The female died when she surprised two of our foot soldiers searching for the supply of lactic fluid.' The Doctor's voice was changing into a deep and sinister whisper. 'The ration was secure, of course. Vulnerable only when in transit.'

'So today they had a go at the carriage,' said Martha,

her fingers closing on a large paperweight. 'And this time they killed themselves.'

'Desperation. Days without rest. Hunger. These things weaken the mind as well as the body.' The voice had become as inhuman and vile as the rest of him. 'I, however, am Felic, of the analyst caste. I am better fed. Strong enough to maintain a complex impersonation. And strong enough to kill you…'

'Please…' Martha turned her back on him, clutched the paperweight tight in her shaking hands. 'Just make it quick.' She braced herself for the scuffle of its claw-like feet on the floorboards, praying she had enough time to react when—

But already Felic was rushing forward. She turned round, swinging the paperweight with all her strength. The smooth white stone cracked against the Zygon's fleshy temple. It hissed in pain, the blow making it stagger and fall off balance into the bookshelf. Martha tried to run past it, but it raised its foot to trip her. She fell to the floor with a hoarse yell, tried to clamber away out of reach, but now Felic had hold of her foot. She writhed in its grip, shouted out, trying to pull free…

And then the door swung open. 'Before you go, Henry…?' Martha looked up to find a man with a shovel staring at the Zygon in shocked disbelief. 'Saints preserve us…'

Martha was about to scream for him to help her. But she didn't need to. The man raised his shovel and brought it down on the Zygon's arm. The creature gasped with pain and Martha finally twisted free of its gnarled fingers. She heard hard, metallic blows rain down on her attacker, awful grunts and scrapes and gurgles.

Then the sounds stopped.

Martha got up, and helped her rescuer stagger back out through the door. Despite his exertions, his face was sickly white, his black moustaches trembling with every heaving breath.

'Thank you,' she said, and closed the hut door. 'Mr...?'

'Chisholm. Howard Chisholm.' He turned back to the hut. 'I thought that was Lord Haleston crashing about in there. What *was* that thing?'

'Clever.' She secured the door with both its bolts. 'And nasty.'

'Never saw a beast like it.'

'Early days yet.' Martha looked up at him. 'There are more of them. Lots more. And it sounds like they're planning something over at Goldspur.'

'I beg your pardon?' He frowned. 'Young lady, I don't know quite what that thing was in there, but—'

'Look, we don't have time for the whole "young lady" bit right now, OK?' Martha grabbed hold of his arms and looked into his eyes. 'If you want to do the full-on gallantry thing, there are a lot more young ladies over at Goldspur. You saw that thing in there...' She raised her eyebrows. 'Do you want *them* to see one too?'

'My wife's at Goldspur...' Chisholm's brow furrowed. 'The Beast's all quiet and soundly secured. I'll round up the chaps.'

'And then we must get the Doctor back. He'll know what to do.' Martha stared about. 'Where *is* Lord Haleston?'

'I was looking for him, I couldn't... Wait.' Chisholm pointed to the adjacent hillside. 'Look!' Romand's car was ascending the path to the main road, and there was Haleston sat beside him in the passenger seat.

'We've got to get after him,' Martha said. 'He won't be expecting trouble.'

'After a day like this one,' muttered Chisholm, following this most unusual woman down the hillside, 'I doubt any of us know *what* to expect.'

'*Martha!*'

The Doctor was jerked awake by a pulse of power, shocking through his body. For a couple of moments he stared round blankly at his surroundings. Then the familiar alien pulse of the Zygon ship crept into his ears.

He was slumped in a kind of narrow stall made of the same fleshy, fibrous stuff as the rest of the craft. Spaghetti cabling ran up and down the wall behind him, and some of it was looped loosely round his wrists and ankles; it must have been holding him in place while Felic ran around the Lakes impersonating him. But now...

'Body-print mechanism fused,' the Doctor murmured, wondering what must have happened to his replica to break their connection. The last thing he'd seen before blacking out was his own, living reflection; Felic had put on a Time Lord body as casually as the Doctor might put on an overcoat.

'I'm going to visit your friend, Doctor,' his doppelganger had said. 'I'm going to rescue the person closest to you and see if she knows the difference.'

'Ha! No problem. You'll never master our secret handshake.'

'You'd better hope she doesn't guess I'm an imposter.' The Doctor's own smile had dazzled back at him. 'If she does, she's dead.'

'What's happened to you, Felic,' the Doctor breathed. 'What happened to Martha?'

Suddenly something tugged at his leg, and he gasped in surprise. Molly Melton was looking up at him, unkempt and teary-eyed.

'Help me,' she said.

'Should I?' the Doctor asked suspiciously. 'Are you really her – Molly Melton?'

'You know my name?' There was nothing fake about the tears the girl had been crying.

'If you're real and you're walking about, that can only mean that someone wearing your form must have…' He thought of the sickly Zygon children in the lab, pictured others still roaming the land, and shut his eyes sadly.

'Must've gone.'

'I don't know where I am,' said Molly sadly. 'I woke up and I'm lost and... please. Who are you? What *is* this place?'

'I'm the Doctor.' He passed her a hanky from his coat pocket and crouched beside her. 'And we've both been stuck in a Zygon body-print resource bank.' He caught her puzzled expression and smiled. 'Put another way, it's a place where nasty orange trolls make perfect copies of people. They wear a person's body as a disguise, see, so no one knows they aren't really human at all.'

Molly blinked. 'I think I know something you don't,' she said solemnly.

'Eh?'

The girl's pale blue eyes gleamed. 'I can show you, if you'll give me a penny.'

'Got change for a sixpence?' the Doctor asked, fishing out a coin from his pocket and dropping it into her palm. 'It's fine, you can owe me. Lead on.'

'All right.' She took a few steps away from the fleshy booth he stood in and smiled mischievously. 'We're here.'

The Doctor gave her a sideways look. Then he stepped out warily and saw that he was in a long, shadowy corridor filled with similar stalls. 'Dear old Mrs U,' he noted, walking along the line. 'And Lunn! Of course, if your spy in the camp's on starvation rations, let him impersonate someone lying in bed all day. Oh, and here's poor, faint-hearted Mrs Lunn. But who else is…'

His voice trailed off as he saw Molly pointing into the shadows further down the corridor. He joined her and saw who – or rather what – was perched improbably in the next stall. And the next… and the next…

'Oh, no,' he whispered, putting both hands to his temples. 'Why didn't I think? Why didn't I consider the obvious!'

'This corridor goes on for miles,' Molly informed him helpfully. 'There's so many of them—'

'We've got to do something.' The Doctor grabbed hold of Molly's hand. 'The Zygons can be anywhere, everywhere, hiding in plain view. We've got to get out of here, right now!'

As the carriage bumped her bones along the dark country lanes, Martha decided that if she ever got back to her own time she would write a book called *Travel in the Edwardian Era*. It would be a short book – OUCH in capital letters followed by fifty pages of bad language.

Then the ornate stone archway that marked the entrance to Goldspur loomed up from the moonlit darkness, and a thrill of nerves went through Martha's stomach. Her heart was pounding a rhythm in sympathy with the chorus of horse hooves on the dirt track. Beside her, Chisholm was cradling his shotgun, lost in thoughts that were perhaps too grim for him to share with 'one of the weaker sex'. Martha sighed, and wondered how he'd react to some of the stories she could tell *him*.

Their carriage was the first in the convoy, and the driver took them right to the front of the house. All the lights were on, and Martha waited for a curious face to appear at one of the many windows, or for Chivvers to open the door in his stoic fashion. But she saw no one.

Martha got out of the carriage herself rather than wait for the footman to open the door for her. She looked around nervously. The din of carriage wheels and hooves as they ground against the pebbled driveway carried through the night, a real racket.

But it didn't seem to bother the herd of cows that now came meandering out of the night, crossing the lawns and heading nonchalantly for the house like they were calling round for dinner. Some of the hunting party had noticed now, and were swapping bemused glances. Some of the horses skittered nervously.

'Dashed strange behaviour,' noted Chisholm, as more cattle came lumbering round from either side of the house. Martha suddenly saw they were advancing almost in formation. Ranged with the others they described a loose semi-circle around the hunting party...

Lord Haleston looked at Romand with some consternation as he drove along a narrow, leafy lane. Darkness had all but fallen, and the Rover's electric lights did little to dispel the gloom. Nevertheless, Romand kept up an alarmingly high speed.

Haleston cleared his throat indignantly. 'Forgive me, Monsieur Romand, but I fail to see how this can possibly be a better route to Goldspur.'

'It is better for my tyres,' said Romand, with an apologetic smile. 'Less rutted, yes?'

'I appreciate that, as I appreciated your offer of a lift,' said Haleston patiently. 'But really, there is a great deal to be done—'

'Wait. What is that?' Romand frowned, pointed to something sitting in the road ahead. As the car slowed down, Haleston recognised the large English Mastiff even before he saw the blackened patch on its back.

'That's Teazel. Edward Lunn's dog.'

'He is far from home,' Romand observed.

'We'll take him along with us.' Haleston twisted round to shift the heavy film camera from the rear seat, then remembered his manners. 'Er… do you have a blanket? If the dog is wet you may wish to cover—'

'It is of no consequence,' Romand told him curtly, as the dog trotted towards them. 'Not when matters of such importance abound.'

'Indeed,' said Haleston, opening the rear door and allowing the dog to settle silently in the back. 'For a start, I must send word to the King that we have captured the Beast of Westmorland.'

'You have already informed his equerry, yes?' Romand interrupted, as the car pulled jerkily away. 'My attendance at the function will be approved?'

'Yes, I sent my houndsman to Stormsby with my proposals. I do not foresee any difficulty there. Meantime, I must inform my guests at Goldspur that those in the hunting party are all well, I must check my wife has made all the arrangements for receiving the King the day after the ceremony...' Haleston cleared his throat. 'So – if a more direct route could be taken, you see, it really would be best all round.'

'Ah, but we would never have found Teazel here, had we not come this way,' said Romand. 'Perhaps things happen for a reason, hmm...?'

Haleston did his best to remain calm as the dark scenery sped by. But then he recognised a distinctive junction. 'Good heavens, man! We're practically in Kelmore! Kindly turn around at once!'

Romand braked, and Haleston grunted with satisfaction as the car began to slow. But then he realised the man was reacting only because the road ahead was blocked by milling cattle. Nine or ten Friesians were looking over languidly in the light of the electric lanterns.

Angrily, Haleston stood up in his seat. 'Where the devil did this lot come from?'

'I do not know,' said Romand. 'But I know where they will be going...'

Haleston stared in horror as Romand's features started to shimmer and melt in a fierce red light. The man's neck swelled. Nodules grew out of the blazing flesh.

Quaking with fear, Haleston scrambled down from the car and fumbled with the rear door. 'Teazel!' he gasped. 'Quickly, boy…'

But as he forced open the door, the film camera tumbled out and hit the track in front of him. The wooden lid cracked loose.

And a duelling pistol clattered out from inside.

The squat, malevolent demon in the driver's seat hissed in anger. Haleston reached for the weapon – but Teazel jumped down on top of it, barking fiercely. The Mastiff too had become engulfed in the same, sinister glare. Teazel's form was twisting, *changing*…

'No…' Haleston shook his head, feebly. 'It isn't possible, it isn't…'

He turned and started to run towards the cattle. If he could only put them between him and the demons…

But now the cattle too were aglow. Haleston was trying to push past but the same evil fit was upon them, their bodies consumed with unearthly fire as their bovine forms twisted into something *alien*… the monstrous kin of those things in the car.

'I'm going mad,' Haleston croaked, staring round wildly. 'This can't be happening… Such creatures do not exist!'

He shut his eyes and tried to will the apparitions away, even as gnarled fingers closed on his throat.

EIGHTEEN

'OK, this is officially weird,' said Martha as the cattle closed in. Like the rest of the hunting party, she found herself being driven back towards the front steps of the house.

And then, like something out of a cartoon, the cows reared up and stood on their hind legs. A dull red glow suffused their black-and-white hides.

'It's a trap!' Martha shouted. 'We've got to get out of here!'

Chisholm swung round and stared at her in horror. 'More of those orange creatures—?'

'I didn't know they could take animal shapes,' she cried, kicking herself for not even considering the possibility. 'Come on, while they're still changing, run!' She tried to lead the charge herself, but many of the men had already fallen to their knees in terror as a dozen squat Zygon silhouettes lunged out from the crimson

currents of energy. She started to push between two of
the morphing creatures, but a clawed foot lashed out
against her ankle and sent her stumbling backwards
into Chisholm.

Then the firing started, as one of the men gave the
nearest Zygon both barrels of his shotgun. The creature
gave a bestial screech and staggered back – but, before
the man could reload, two more Zygons pressed their
clawing hands against his face. His screams almost
drowned the boom of another gun firing – this time
harmlessly into the air as a Zygon knocked the barrel
upwards, then smashed the face of the firer with the
back of its fist.

'Stay behind me, Miss Jones,' Chisholm shouted,
backing away up the steps.

But Martha was already scaling them full pelt. She
was about to hammer on the door, to yell for someone
to let them inside, when the door opened.

A Zygon towered in the doorway. Its scabrous arm
was held tight around Ian's neck. The alien's dark eyes
burned into Martha's as the claw-like hand moved
slowly towards the terrified boy's tear-stained cheek…

'Everyone stop!' Martha screamed at the top of her
lungs. The men turned in shock and surprise.

'Drop your weapons.' The piggy eyes of the Zygon in
the doorway flitted between them, alert to any attack.
'Remain still. If any of you move against us, I will execute
this child – and your females will soon follow.'

'Sorry,' Ian whimpered.

Martha heard shotguns fall to the ground with a clatter, and a gloating hiss of satisfaction from the Zygon before her. 'What are you going to do with us?' she demanded.

The Zygon didn't speak, but its lips twitched in a cruel smile.

Lord Haleston was being led on a nightmare march through dark, wet forest by the inhuman creatures. The cold, Christmas smell of the conifers mingled with a tang of iron as the brutes jostled him along. He was grateful the moonlight was so thin; the demons were easier to accept as mere shadows in the dark.

His senses were still screaming: *Such things cannot exist.* He had studied so many species, classified and ordered so many organisms by their shared characteristics. He had sought and thought to understand life. Now these beasts tormented him not only with their bony grip and whispered threats, but with their very being. Such creatures were a blasphemy against the Creator. They had no place in the living world. They could only be spirits of supernature, denizens of hell.

'How much further?' Haleston asked hoarsely. 'Where are you leading me?'

'Ohhh, to their cunningly hidden underwater spaceship, I should think!'

It was the Doctor's voice, ringing out through the darkness.

Haleston stopped dead in his tracks in a small clearing, and his escorts did the same. One of them spoke in a whispering voice: 'The Doctor has escaped.'

'Yep! I found an underground channel leading from the hillside down to the spaceship in the lake,' the Doctor explained. 'Very clever and surprisingly roomy. Lick of paint might be nice, mind. Where's Martha?'

'The female is of no consequence,' came the deep gurgling reply.

'Sounds like you don't know! That's encouraging.'

Haleston was coming to doubt his senses. 'Doctor, how did you get here ahead of me?'

'Use your loaf, your grace! I didn't. The me you've been dealing with was really one of *them* – more of their clever alien technology.' There was a rustle of foliage; the crack of dead wood somewhere in the dark, and the Zygons stared around as if trying to pinpoint the source of the sound. '*Very* clever. Lord Haleston, have you met Brelarn, Warlord of the Zygons?'

Haleston heard the rasping, angry hiss close behind. 'Show yourself, Doctor.'

'Unfortunately, Brelarn, it was *less* clever to leave your cunningly hidden spaceship more or less unmanned. I could sneak out pretty damned easily. Even Analyst Taro's pushed off.' The Doctor's voice had a harder edge now. 'So I strolled out of your secret tunnel, Brelarn. *Strolled.* I suppose most days you post a couple of cows on guard outside the hidden entrance. Why not? None of the locals would bat an eyelid. But not tonight. Everyone's gone.'

'Be silent,' Brelarn warned him. Silently, he signalled two of his Zygon demons to explore eastwards.

'So, deserted spaceship, hardly any guards…' Now the Doctor's voice seemed to come from the west. 'Makes me think that some last-ditch, opportunist attempt to save your Zygon skins is afoot tonight. Something big enough for you to risk showing your hand to the humans…'

'I will kill *this* human unless you show yourself,' Brelarn rasped.

'Come off it! When you've gone to so much trouble to get him? After you've spent so long spying inside his house and reading his diaries? No, whatever you're up to, you need Haleston. You need him baaaaad. But why?'

'The King!' Haleston shouted, feeling sick. 'In my vanity, I arranged for Romand to attend a private function with the King. But Romand is one of them.'

'Is that it, Brelarn?' Beneath the Doctor's voice, stealthy sounds of movement carried through the forest – seemingly behind them now – and another two Zygons lumbered away to investigate. 'You want to take Edward the Seventh's body print and put a Zygon on the throne?'

'The British King is a figurehead, nothing more,' Brelarn sneered. 'But were he to be assassinated…'

'Then it's not the King you want,' said the Doctor, his words cutting coldly through the darkness. 'Of course. It's his funeral, isn't it?'

The gun in the camera, thought Haleston. *So 'Romand' can smuggle the weapon inside...*

'Imagine the outcry should this so-called "Uncle of Europe" be shot dead,' Brelarn agreed. 'World leaders will gather for the funeral, and there they will meet and mingle with the politicians of this country.'

'The Prime Minister... my colleagues, my friends...' Haleston sank to his knees with dreadful realisation, wincing as the Zygon claws dug in harder. 'You want to use me to get to them?'

'Or the likeness of you, anyway. That's why they needed you from the start, to reel in old Asquith and company.' Suddenly, the Doctor appeared between two skeletal elms. 'Abduction, death, manipulation, deceit. Just your typical Zygon Saturday night.'

'We have already taken Haleston's dwelling,' hissed Brelarn. 'It will become a Zygon stronghold, a place where we may learn your ludicrous social rituals and study the leaders we will replace. Our imposture will be noticed by none... until it is too late.'

Why is it only talking? thought Haleston. *Why not attack the Doctor now...?*

Then he saw what the Zygon must have seen. The same little girl he'd seen through his telescope that morning – a slight, sinister figure creeping up behind the Doctor in the thin lick of moonlight. *The Zygons' familiar*, he realised, and opened his mouth to shout a warning.

Too late. The girl thrust her hand out to the Doctor's back, and he gasped with pain, staggered and fell out of sight amid much crashing of foliage. The girl followed him.

'Excellent, my child,' Brelarn hissed, striding after them. 'But do not kill him. His ingenuity may yet—'

The Zygon Warlord broke off, held still. The crashing in the foliage was growing louder. For a split second Haleston felt a tremble in the cold, damp ground beneath his knees.

Then a charging bull burst between the two elms and into the little clearing. Huge head lowered, it butted Brelarn aside into one of his aides. More cattle trampled into the clearing, their hooves cracking over sticks and Zygon limbs alike. One of Haleston's guards lunged forwards, arm outstretched to sting the nearest. Haleston threw himself forwards, broke free of the grip of his remaining guard and struggled away. The madness continued as a horse came galloping into the clearing. It reared up, and Haleston ducked its flailing legs. A Zygon wasn't so lucky – an iron-shod hoof cracked into its skull and it staggered backwards into the forest's shadows.

Haleston ducked beneath a branch and ran desperately through the undergrowth, tearing through bracken, stumbling over rotting logs. He couldn't allow himself to be recaptured, but where was he? Where in God's name could he find safety—?

'This way, your lordship,' came a hoarse whisper, close by.

There was no mistaking the French accent. Romand was standing just behind him.

'Keep away,' Haleston hissed, staring into the man's dark eyes. 'I won't be part of your filthy plans, d'you hear?'

He made to run again, but a Zygon had emerged from the wooded shadows, blocking his retreat.

Romand knocked Haleston to the ground with a kick to the back of his knees. 'I have him,' he told the Zygon coldly. 'He will not escape a second time, I'll see to that. Now, quickly – find the Doctor.'

The Zygon hissed its understanding and lumbered away. Haleston stared up at Romand with hatred.

Then, to his surprise, the Frenchman puffed out his cheeks and gave a low whistle. 'Happily it seems I have fooled you both, no?' he murmured, helping Haleston to his feet. 'I am the real Claude Romand. I was, how do you say… *ambushed* by these creatures as I drove along the road this afternoon.'

Haleston heaved a shaky sigh of relief. 'Yes, they got me in much the same way.'

'Then let us vow they shall get us no more!' Romand clapped Haleston on the back. 'Please. Come with me to a place of safety, yes?'

Haleston allowed himself to be led away through the murky forest and out onto landscaped lawns. He recognised the toothy silhouette of the half-ruined Kelmore Manor against the starry sky, as Romand steered him towards a red-brick cottage. As they got closer, Haleston found his fellow survivors had got there ahead of him. Sir Albert Morton, back from the dead, was clutching his sobbing wife in a tight embrace. A battered-looking Edward Lunn clung to his wife, darling Cynthia, and the pair were joined by the stalwart Teazel, panting happily at his master's feet. Mrs Unswick, from the Lodge, was slumped on the ground with a bottle of smelling salts. And there was the Doctor, lifting the young girl who'd sham-attacked him from the back of a large, black horse.

'Claude! Lord Haleston, there you are!' The Doctor gave them a beaming grin and started gabbling nineteen to the dozen. 'Glad you could make it. As you can see, touching little reunion here – turns out it was Sir Albert's Zygon double who was killed in the Skarasen's spree, while the real McCoy slept through the whole thing. He and his wife plan to celebrate by spending the rest of the night in the manor's wine cellars looking after young Molly, Mrs U, Mr Lunn and the charming Cynthia here – out of sight and hopefully out of reach, but with Teazel to protect them on the off-chance.' He looked wistful for a moment, staring into space. 'So, no need to crack open a bottle of the 1811 Riesling just yet, though it would certainly knock out the nerves with style…'

'I can't stay cosseted here,' said Lunn, starting forward a little unsteadily. 'I want to help.'

Cynthia placed an anxious hand on his shoulder. 'You barely managed the journey through the forest, my love.'

'Our son could be at the mercy of those monsters.' His voice was hoarse with pain. 'I can't stand back and do nothing.'

'You'll be doing nothing ever again if you don't try to rest,' the Doctor told him. 'I'll see that Ian's all right.'

'And *I'll* feel better with another man about the place!' called Mrs U, the faintest sparkle returning to her eyes.

'Lord Haleston, what news on the Beast of Westmorland?' asked the Doctor.

'But that's been taken care of, you…' Haleston felt suddenly sick. 'Of course, I was forgetting. It *wasn't* you at all, was it?'

'No. It wasn't.' The Doctor looked grave. 'Has the Skarasen been secured?'

Haleston nodded. 'Tranquilised, chained up and half-buried on the lakeshore at Templewell.'

'Tranquilised, eh?' The Doctor considered the news. 'My little device worked then. Brilliant! Terrific! Not to mention, absolutely disastrous.' He scowled. 'With the Skarasen asleep they can operate to restore its control matrix, bring it back under their control…'

'Operate?' Romand broke in. 'Surely the attempt on King Edward's life will be their priority?'

'These Zygon creatures are mad,' said Haleston bitterly. 'To embark on such a scheme... they *must* be mad!'

'Mad? No. Desperate, maybe. Shrewd...' The Doctor nodded vigorously. 'Yeah, shrewd's the word. Take over the Cabinet and you wield real political control in Britain. Nobble the leaders of a dozen more countries at a very big and very posh function, and you stand to take control of most of Europe. Though conquest's just a means to an end in this case. With a tip-top Skarasen and a long-term supply of lactic fluid secured, they'll be set to put the peoples of the world on a programme of climate change and environmental engineering, turn this world into a Zygon paradise.'

'But what you talk of, Doctor...' Romand looked bemused. 'Surely, it is fantasy... a fiction?'

The Doctor looked at him gravely. 'If only it was. You humans have already started the climate changes yourselves...' Suddenly he clapped his hands together, jolting himself back into manic action. 'And what of my plans, you may well ask, now I've effected two very daring escapes, coaxed out the enemy's plans and temporarily traumatised a small army of kidnapped farmyard animals? Well, in the first place – Martha.'

'I last saw her at Templewell while we were subduing the Beast,' said Haleston. 'She... I'm afraid she was in the company of your doppelganger when I left her.'

'Then she escaped from the Lodge…' The Doctor frowned. 'I don't know what happened to Felic, but if he did dupe Martha, chances are she's been taken back there.'

'Or to Goldspur,' Romand reasoned.

'We'll look at the Lodge first, it's closest,' the Doctor announced. 'I need to find her before Brelarn gets any clever ideas about using her against me.'

'I pray we are in time to aid Miss Jones, of course,' said Haleston solemnly. 'But what of the King? He will be arriving at Stormsby tomorrow. He must be warned of this plot.'

'Can you contact him by wire?' asked Lunn.

'For any remote communication I require the proper codes and passwords,' Haleston explained. 'They were changed recently; I have them recorded in my journal at Goldspur, but…'

'That means the Zygons most probably have them too,' said the Doctor. 'They've been snooping through your papers.'

'Then I must go to His Majesty in person!' Haleston declared, staring out towards Stormsby. 'It's a twelve-mile ride from here…'

But the Doctor shook his head. 'Your grace, you're the Zygons' trump card. Brelarn will be watching out for you.'

'Then we ride in force, together.' Lunn threw up his arms. 'Damn it all, man, we can't let—'

'Look,' the Doctor cut in, 'no offence, I'm sure he's a lovely king, in fact, he *is* a lovely king. If you like kings… Anyway, we haven't got the time to trek over to Stormsby and warn him right now. The Zygons are most likely healing the Skarasen as we speak, and if they succeed, old Edward won't be safe anywhere – believe me.' He frowned. 'No. No, we've got to stop this danger at source.'

Romand raised an eyebrow. 'What would you suggest, Doctor?'

'Oh, I dunno, I'll think of something.' He suddenly smiled. 'While there are stout-hearted men with rested horses and a ridiculous optimism that good will prevail, all is not lost!' The Doctor threw an arm round their shoulders and steered them away towards the stables. 'We must get to the Lodge. *Allons-y*, gentlemen – we've got a world to save!'

NINETEEN

Martha had encountered several alien creatures in her time, and was no stranger to their evil agendas. Yet the Zygons were the first monsters she'd met who forced their prisoners into playing cards.

It was a surreal situation. The ladies of the house, even the maids, were sat miserably in the drawing room playing games like Bridge and Bezique and Bid Whist, while Zygons stood about, watching in silence. One or two of the creatures were slumped against the wall. Either the ridiculous rules had sapped their will to live or they were suffering badly from the rationing. Martha only wished a few more would keel over – that way, they might just stand a chance of escaping this madness.

Martha's ignorance of card games had left her to endure a different role-play with Ian and Victor – that of taking a make-believe afternoon tea. She was on slippery ground there, too, but Victor was proving knowledgeable and she was trying to nod in all the right places. Ian just sat there, staring sullenly into space.

'So you see,' Victor was explaining to their impassive Zygon observer, 'if one is drinking tea while seated at a table, the proper manner is to raise only the teacup, placing it back into the saucer between sips. However, if one is attending a buffet...'

Suddenly the Zygon reacted, but not to Victor's words. Martha saw it was holding some kind of device in its clawed hand. It retired to the double doors and held it to the side of its oversized head.

'This is lunacy,' muttered Victor. 'Teaching monsters to drink tea?'

'Suppose it's not enough just to look like someone in this day and age,' Martha reflected. 'Think about it, everything's about manners and etiquette. The people they've chosen to impersonate so far have been shunning the social scene.'

Ian nodded. 'Like my mother, always in her room.'

'And your father, on his sickbed,' said Victor.

'Right,' Martha agreed. 'They must have been observing people like the Doctor and Mrs Unswick to get the gist of their characters, but they're not high society. Now the Zygons must be setting their sights on people who are, and they'll stand out like sore thumbs unless they can pick up some of the social graces.'

'It's the Prime Minister and his Cabinet they're after,' said Ian quietly. 'Must be. Victor and I found a telegram inviting them here. My mother…' He broke off. 'The thing pretending to be my mother must have sent it.'

'Probably took the contact details from Lord Haleston's diary,' Martha realised. 'Makes sense. Entertain the Cabinet, get them nice and relaxed and off guard, then steal their bodies…' She saw how upset Ian looked and gave his hand a reassuring squeeze. 'Look, at least you know for sure your mum's alive, and your dad too.' She glanced at Victor. 'Even Teazel. The Doctor told me the Zygons need to update their body prints every so often or they can't stay in disguise.' Martha sighed. 'I only hope that means they've had to keep *him* alive too.'

Now it was Ian's turn to squeeze her hand, and she smiled.

'I wonder why I'm not permitted to mingle with the chaps in the dining hall?' Victor wondered. 'Ever since that hell-hound sent me to sleep, they've kept me in here with the ladies.'

'Don't forget they've got hidden bugs all over the place.' She raised her eyebrows. 'Perhaps you have a reputation.'

Victor blushed. 'Miss Jones, please…'

The Zygon by the double doors lowered the device from his ears and marched over to another observing the card games. 'Algor reports that repairs to the Skarasen are being undertaken by Taro,' it reported. 'The operation should take only hours to complete. And once a fresh supply of lactic fluid is secured, we have permission to consume all emergency rations.'

At this, one of the slumping Zygons seemed to revive. 'When will the next batch be sent?'

'It will be sent at oh-five-hundred hours,' hissed the Zygon in the know.

'We shall feast,' rumbled another of the creatures.

'Er, excuse me?' Martha called. 'We could use some extra rations too. It's close to eleven, been a long time since that rotten breakfast your friend cooked me…'

The Zygon lumbered towards her, its dark eyes bright as berries. 'When the carriage has delivered our food,' it hissed, 'it will take unnecessary humans to be stored in our ship.'

Martha tried to look unbothered. 'And then you'll get busy replicating, yeah? Ready for the big Zygon dress rehearsal.'

Suddenly, the double doors opened, and two Zygon guards led Chisholm inside. 'Do not speak,' one of them warned him. 'Or the females will be damaged.'

Several of the ladies burst into tears. 'Howard,' Lady Chisholm sobbed. 'Oh, Howard, please don't let them hurt us…'

Chisholm stared dismally round the room, but said nothing. His moustache was all-consuming, but it was a fair bet there was a stiff upper lip somewhere beneath it.

'They are unharmed,' the Zygon went on. 'But if you do not serve us, they shall be destroyed.'

The two Zygons led him from the room and closed the door.

'Making their point before our taxi-carriage arrives,' Martha supposed. 'Now we know why you're in with us, Victor. You're the only single man here. They must think some tame humans might be a useful social support to them—'

'So they bag them by threatening their wives.' Victor scowled. 'Animals.'

'And once they've fed and got their strength back,' said Ian gloomily, 'we won't stand a chance of getting away.'

'What chance would you say we stood now?' Victor gestured around them. 'The doors are guarded and they've locked all the windows.'

Ian shook his head a faction. 'The lock doesn't work properly on one of the patio doors,' he whispered. 'If you shake the handle in just the right way, it ought to open.'

'Oh, yes?' Victor frowned. 'And how would you know that, urchin?'

'Something I discovered yesterday while sneaking in to avoid the wrath of Nanny,' Ian confessed.

'Well, God bless Nanny's ire and your inquisitive nature,' said Victor. He looked at Martha. 'We're in with a chance, Miss Jones.'

'Perhaps we are.' Martha looked furtively round at the sheer volume of Zygon guards. 'We've had afternoon tea. Time for something more substantial…'

* * *

Bent forward in the saddle, his heels pressed hard to Arthur's flanks, the Doctor was on the ride of his life. The wind howled in his ears and teased tears from his eyes as the horse shot like a dark arrow across the moonlit fields and lanes. Romand was following on Mrs Unswick's gelding, while Haleston rode to the rear on a stallion borrowed from Sir Albert's stables.

Occasionally they passed resting cattle and staring sheep, and gave them a wide berth. The Doctor thought crossly of the way the Zygon had appeared apparently from nowhere when he'd first summoned the Skarasen, the way he'd blithely burbled out his plans to Daisy the Zygon Cow up on Kelmore Hill…

'You idiot,' he told himself.

He supposed that if you were on reduced rations, taking the form of a mute herd animal was a good way to conserve precious energy. Always out and about, you could observe the local customs, gain intelligence, set up communications relays and supply dumps; build a secret infrastructure that allowed you to operate in plain view of your enemies, without them raising an eyebrow.

He'd forgotten how cunning Zygons could be.

The Doctor pulled up on Arthur's reins, straightened in the saddle to slow down his steed as they rounded a copse of trees. He wiped his eyes and stared about, trying to get his bearings.

Then he saw a lumpy silhouette, about a hundred metres away. A mute sentinel in the field. 'Zygon,' he murmured, urging Arthur back round behind the copse before they were spotted. His companions rode up alongside. 'No good,' he said quietly. 'Might be others. We'll have to go back and circle round to the next field.'

'And if there's a Zygon in that field too?' Haleston wondered.

The Doctor looked at him. 'Then we'll try the next. We'll get to the Lodge, find out if Martha's there.'

Leaving Haleston and Romand to swap glances, he rode back the same way they'd come.

It took hours, and many times they had to turn away or outwait a Zygon patrol. But finally, the Lodge came into view, nestling in the hillside ahead of them.

'Be careful,' the Doctor told Haleston and Romand. 'Like Goldspur, this is a Zygon outpost now.'

But as the Doctor urged his exhausted horse along the wooded track that wound round to the Lodge itself, he saw nothing sinister. The night was silent save for the whistle of the wind, the rustling of branches and the mournful hoot of a hunting owl.

The front of the Lodge came into view. A single light burned in the hall window. A large, covered carriage was parked to the side of the house.

'Someone's still up at this late hour,' the Doctor mused, jumping down from his horse. 'Shall we find out who?' He advanced on the front door, reached inside his jacket pocket for the sonic screwdriver – then realised his double had taken it to trigger the adapted activator. With a sigh, he turned to Haleston and Romand. 'Anyone got a hairpin?'

But suddenly the door was flung open and a Zygon burst out from inside, its stinging claws swiping the air as it lunged for the Doctor's face.

The Doctor hurled himself backwards out of the way, but the Zygon kept coming, leapt onto him. He gasped as the breath was knocked from his body. Haleston and Romand both tried to drag the Zygon away, but the creature shrugged them off. It tore at the Doctor's coat and jacket, ripped at his shirt, trying to send its sting directly into the flesh of his chest…

Then there was a loud thud, and the Zygon went rigid. A further thump and it slumped forwards, lifeless to the ground. The Doctor stared up in alarm as a thin, wraithlike figure loomed over him: a bony woman whose hard, angular features were livid with bruises. She was wielding a poker, and her black eyes held a frantic look.

'How do *you* like it?' she shouted at the fallen Zygon. 'How do you like being on the receiving end? Eh?'

'It's all right, Miss Flock.' Haleston put a gallant arm about the woman while Romand prised the poker from her grip. 'Are there any more of these creatures in the house?'

'I don't think so.' She shook her head, clearly in shock. 'It left me for dead. I woke up, crawled away… I've been hiding upstairs for hours, and all the time, I could hear that *thing* talking to itself in the sitting room. It didn't know I was here. And I didn't dare move – until I heard your voices outside. And then, when it got distracted—'

'You took your chance. Thanks.' The Doctor sat bolt upright. 'Have you seen Martha Jones?'

Miss Flock went lemon lipped. 'That girl *was* here, but she's gone. She, Mr Meredith, the boy, they all cleared off…' She started to sob. 'Ian Lunn was in my care!'

'There, there,' said Haleston awkwardly. 'I'm sure he's all right.'

'But don't you see?' the nanny bawled. 'If he isn't, that's me out of a job!'

'Nothing like a sense of perspective, is there?' said the Doctor, crouching to inspect the Zygon.

Romand eyed it nervously. 'It is dead, Doctor, yes?'

'Yep. Already weak from dehydration…' He looked at Miss Flock. 'What was the Zygon downstairs talking *about*?'

'It was babbling,' she told him. 'Something about the last of the supplies, getting the carriage ready… Babbling.'

'Or else talking into their hidden communicator, receiving instructions.' The Doctor got up and went to inspect the carriage. 'Lord Haleston, can you fetch me a light? And Romand, perhaps you'd search the house – carefully – and shout if you find anything interesting.'

Romand inclined his head. Haleston strode away, and

the Doctor crossed to the carriage. Inside were a number of large, squat objects that looked like a cross between a tree stump and a pizza. They felt warm to the touch.

'What are they?' asked Haleston uneasily, returning with a paraffin lamp.

'Portable larders, I think,' breathed the Doctor. 'Probably packed with lactic fluid from the Skarasen, it keeps the Zygons alive.' He picked up one of the stumps and saw a puckered line like a scar running down one side, secured with a line of fleshy staples. They felt dry and taut to his touch. 'Time release mechanism,' he surmised. 'As these strands dry out, they peel away, but until then they'll keep sticky Zygon fingers out till feeding time. And it looks like we're getting close…

Then Romand's hoarse cry carried from an upstairs window. 'Doctor, Lord Haleston! Quickly!' He looked down at them helplessly. 'I can see lights on the road… quite a few of them. Turning onto the driveway.'

Miss Flock stared out into the darkness. 'Something's coming,' she said.

TWENTY

Martha watched the ornate hands of the grandfather clock tick heavily round towards five. Soon it would be dawn. The ladies lay slumped in their chairs, some drifting in uneasy sleep, others still wide-eyed and clutching their cards like little scraps of comfort. But the Zygons remained stubbornly on guard. They had a kind of rota system going on, each taking a turn to rest before resuming duty. And every attempt to shuffle closer to the French windows was thwarted with a hissed warning, a *Do not move*, or a *Remain still*.

Martha leaned over to Victor and Ian. 'If we're going to make a break, it had better be soon,' she whispered. 'We need a distraction.'

Bang on cue, the doors crashed open and a large, imposing Zygon burst inside. It was the one she'd surprised in Haleston's study, as livid as the scar that ran down the side of its face. More Zygons tumbled inside close on their leader's heels. One of the women screamed, and Lady Chisholm promptly fainted. Martha noticed that even their Zygon guard looked alarmed, turning in consternation.

'Commander Brelarn,' it hissed.

'Is he here?' the scarred Zygon demanded. 'The Doctor, where is he?'

The Doctor. Martha's heart leapt. *He's alive, and causing trouble.* She looked at Victor and Ian while their surprised guard was looking to its superior.

'It's now or never,' she muttered, and darted away towards the heavy drapes that hid the French windows from view. Once there, she stood up so she'd make less of a bulge in the thick velvet, and peeped out to check she hadn't been seen.

Ian gave her a thumbs-up. 'Turn the handle and jostle,' he mouthed at her.

Martha nodded and tried the handle, which squeaked alarmingly.

Then she heard Ian stand up. 'I know where the Doctor is!' he announced.

'Who is this child?' Brelarn wheezed.

'You've got my parents, Mr and Mrs Lunn. I'll tell you where the Doctor is if you let them go.'

'Don't be an idiot, Ian,' Victor snapped. 'I won't let you tell them a thing.'

'Thanks, boys,' muttered Martha, as their overplayed sounds of struggle and some flutters from the ladies masked the door handle's protesting squeals. But the door itself remained shut fast.

'Speak then, child,' snarled Brelarn. He sounded horribly close.

'Come on…' Martha rattled the door as hard as she dared. It wouldn't budge.

'The Doctor, he… he lives over in Horn Lane,' Ian said. 'The small cottage next to the dairy.'

An angry hissing started up. 'What nonsense is this?'

'It's not nonsense,' Ian protested, 'Dr Fenchurch really lives there!'

Martha heaved up on the handle and shook again. 'Come *on*…'

'I do not require a human physician!' roared Brelarn. 'I must have the *Doctor*!'

Ian cried out – just as the door clicked open. Martha peeped anxiously through the drapes and saw Ian sprawled at Brelarn's feet. He winked at her.

'Where is the dark-skinned girl?' the guard demanded.

'Yes, the Doctor's friend, where is she?' Brelarn advanced on Victor, his hand outstretched. 'Answer me, human… *Where is she?*'

'She's *off!*' Martha shouted from the French windows. 'See ya!'

'Retrieve her!' Brelarn boomed.

Martha ran out across the dew-soaked lawn, hoping they would leave Victor and come after her instead.

Maybe then he and Ian could launch an offensive of their own. The cold air stung her skin, and her quick breaths were like puffs of steam about her. She didn't hesitate, running as fast as she could, heading for the front of the house. A couple of carriages waited there, and Romand's car was now parked beside Victor's. Was Romand here, somewhere? She wouldn't get far trying to drive the thing on her own.

Taking a deep breath, she forced her legs to move faster. She had to get away, get help – if she could only find a horse that wasn't lashed up to a carriage and reach the main road, perhaps she could flag someone down. Or maybe she could—

'Martha!' came a delighted roar as she rounded the corner of the house.

Martha skidded to a halt on the pebbled drive. *'Doctor?'*

He was standing a stone's throw away on the lawn beside a bush, apparently alone. 'Oh, Martha, I was so worried! I've been looking for you…'

'Stay back,' she said, suddenly wary. 'I'm not letting you try to kill me again. I mean, how could the Doctor just pop up here?'

'But it's me! It's *really* me. I got out of the Zygon spaceship, I got *everyone* out – Mrs U, Molly Melton, Mr and Mrs Lunn, more cows than you could shake a stick at. Teazel, even…'

'What about Clara?' asked Martha.

'*She* wasn't there,' the Doctor admitted. 'I thought she'd already left the Lodge?'

'Clara didn't leave. She was killed there.'

'Oh, Martha, I'm sorry. I'm so sorry.' The Doctor turned those big, little-boy eyes on her, so impassioned, so full of hurt, so *real*. 'But you know, they're gonna kill so many more people if we let them and—'

'All right, shut up, it *is* you!' Martha ran to him and grabbed him in a tight hug.

He hugged her back and grinned down at her. 'I would have got here sooner but I had some problems with the neighbours. What's the situation in Goldspur?'

As he spoke, he looked over to the house, and so did Martha.

'Ah,' said the Doctor. 'Not good, then. *Never* waste time in a hug.'

The front door hung open. Brelarn was glaring at them from the bottom of the steps, flanked by two large Zygons. More of the creatures were spilling out from inside the house, at least thirty, some dragging human prisoners with them – men and women alike. Despite her fear, Martha felt a pang of relief to see Victor was unharmed and Ian's only obvious injury was a bruise shining on his cheek.

Brelarn's eyes narrowed 'Doctor…'

'Hello again, Brelarn,' the Doctor replied, leaning forward and clasping his hands behind his back. 'Thought I'd offer the Warlord of the Zygons one last chance to stop all this.' He took a step forward, and his voice hardened. 'Let these people go. Go back to your ship. Return to the amber and sleep away the centuries. Wait for your rescue.'

'I have the chance to rescue this world from the fumbling grasp of humanity,' growled Brelarn, clenching his misshapen fist. 'And I shall take it.'

'No, you shan't.' The Doctor shook his head. 'I'll stop you.'

'How can you stop me?' Brelarn sneered. 'One man against the might of the Zygons?'

'You know, Zygon might *might* not be enough.' The Doctor's eyes gleamed dangerously. 'In fact, I think I *might* have found a match for it.' He pulled one hand from behind his back to reveal a long safety match. 'Aha! Here it is.'

Brelarn started walking slowly towards the Doctor. 'You are a prattling fool.'

'Don't make me do this,' the Doctor warned him. Martha watched anxiously as he struck the match against the box he held in his other hand, and it sputtered into life. 'I swear, this is all I need to destroy you.'

A low rattle like laughter sounded in the back of Brelarn's throat. 'You would seek to destroy us with a piece of tiny fire?'

'Ah, but as anyone on this planet will tell you,' the Doctor retorted, 'it's not what you've got, it's what you *do* with it that counts.'

So saying, he shoved the match into the bush behind him and held it there for a few moments. Something in there began to smoke.

Brelarn hesitated in his advance. 'What are you—'

Suddenly, with a piercing whistle, a distress flare flew up into the overcast sky, trailing red vapour. A loud crack echoed round the grounds. Some of the ladies squealed.

Martha watched the skies expectantly. But nothing happened.

The Doctor had shoved his hands in his pockets, his expression hard to read.

Brelarn looked at him. 'You think to stop me with fireworks?'

'It's a start.' The Doctor shrugged. 'Right, who fancies a snack while we're waiting for the next bit?' He pulled his hands from his pockets, and Martha stared in amazement.

Each hand was jammed full of the root-like phials of Skarasen milk.

'The lactic fluid bars are on me!' yelled the Doctor, throwing the roots at the crowded steps. 'Tuck in, boys and girls!'

Victor quickly stamped on one as it fell, and it burst open in a splash of green goo. Hungry hisses and a sulphurous stink filled the air, as orange hands started clawing for the roots.

'Hey, those are my moves you're nicking,' said Martha, amazed. 'I did that back at the Lodge.'

The Doctor beamed. 'Great minds think alike?'

'Or fools seldom differ,' said Martha – as Brelarn charged towards the Doctor with horrible speed. 'Look out!' she yelled.

The Doctor ducked aside just in time, and stuck one of the roots in the Zygon's mouth like a cigar. Then he dug his hands back into his coat pockets – 'Martha, here!' – and tossed another bundle of roots across to her. She caught as many as she could and started lobbing them at the starving Zygons, some of whom were already stooping and stumbling about, trying to scoop up the precious food.

'Do not react!' Brelarn bellowed at his troops. 'You shall be punished.'

'Bad luck, you brute!' Victor shouted, rescuing a young slip of a thing from the clutch of another drooling Zygon. 'Looks like you've got another mutiny on your hands!'

And, breathlessly, Martha realised he might be right. She watched as two Zygons abandoned their prisoners to fight over the rations, while Chisholm tore free of his own captor, turned, and shoved it down the steps. The Doctor hit the casualty expertly on the head with another of the milk-stuffed roots.

But not all the Zygons were so easily swayed. One man was stung in the face and Lady Chisholm shrieked as alien fists smashed her to the floor. Ian helped the injured man to safety while Chisholm went back for his wife, kicking her attacker aside.

Brelarn roared again, an inhuman, throaty, whooping sound. His eyes were blazing red and he was out for blood now. Again he grabbed for the Doctor. Martha ran up behind and kicked the Zygon's ankle, so that it turned and swiped at her instead.

'Get out of here!' the Doctor yelled at Victor and Ian as they hauled the last man and girl out of danger's reach. 'Run, and don't stop running.'

'That goes for us too, Doctor!' Martha shouted, dodging clear of the Zygon commander's scything claws.

'Your attempts to thwart me are futile,' Brelarn rasped. 'My crew will regain their senses, and I shall recapture the humans before they can fetch help. You have done nothing but provide a pathetic distraction.'

'That's right, Brelarn,' said the Doctor, a sad look in his eyes. 'But it all goes to show, an army marches on its stomach, doesn't it?' He pointed past the Zygon to the gardens. 'Just ask *these* boys.'

And suddenly, Martha realised she could hear hoof-beats. She whirled round – but didn't believe what she was seeing. Soldiers. There must have been twenty soldiers on horseback, each dressed in red jackets piped with yellow, wearing funny black hats. Their swords rattled by their sides as their horses thundered over the ornamental gardens.

'Here comes the cavalry.' She looked at the Doctor in amazement. 'How many times do you get to say that and *mean* it?'

'The Eighth King's Royal Scottish Hussars, to be precise,' said the Doctor. 'Waiting outside the grounds. That flare I sent up was the signal for them to charge.'

Brelarn stared at the Doctor, impotent with rage. 'You tricked me.'

'I tried to warn you,' the Doctor shouted as the hoof-beats grew louder. 'You're a threat to the King. They'll have orders to kill. Surrender to them now, Brelarn, while there's still time.'

But the Zygon Warlord was already lumbering back towards his fellows, barking out instructions, bringing order to the disarray. At his command, two Zygons crossed to an abandoned carriage and upturned it to use as cover. More Zygons were spilling from the house with shotguns liberated from the hunting party. Some took up defensive positions on the steps.

The cavalry were closing fast. With a defiant, gurgling roar, Brelarn ran towards the captain's horse, one hand outstretched to sting it. Martha looked away as the captain brought down his sword on the alien's arm...

Then one of the Zygons opened fire on the Doctor. The shot tore away half of the bush beside him.

'Out of here,' the Doctor shouted, grabbing Martha by the hand and hauling her clear of the battlefield. As she raced to keep up with him, she heard a horrible hotchpotch of battle sounds: war cries and gunfire, the *thunk* of steel biting into flesh, bloodcurdling, inhuman screams...

'Told you I had problems with the neighbours,' the Doctor shouted over the blast of the shotguns. 'The cavalry turned up at the Lodge, out of the blue.'

She grabbed hold of him, stopped him running. 'How come?'

'Edward Lunn. The human Edward Lunn.' He smiled. 'The *brilliantly* human Edward Lunn. Injured from his fall, gone through hell and alien abduction, but 'cause kid, king and country's in trouble, he gallops full pelt through the night to the barracks at Stormsby and tells all the King's men we need help.'

They set off again for the cover of the wooded drive. 'Did you see Nanny Flock?' asked Martha.

The Doctor nodded. 'She saved my life with a poker.'

Martha looked at him in dismay. 'Does that mean I have to like her now?'

He grinned. 'Nah.'

They ran on, but suddenly a woman's screams compelled her to look back through the trees at the carnage. The churned up lawn was littered with Zygon bodies. She saw Cynthia Lunn being cut down by a mounted soldier, while Edward was trying to stave off two more using his shotgun as a club.

Martha looked away, sickened. 'They must have thought that if they looked human they might stand a chance of slipping away...'

'Yeah, Haleston warned the soldier-boys something like that might happen.' The Doctor's face was ashen as the early morning light as the sounds of conflict died away. 'They assured him they wouldn't be put off.'

'How do you know there aren't other Zygons about?' Martha said quietly.

'Oh, there could well be a few,' he admitted. 'But I've emptied their body-print resource bank and killed the controls. The Zygons need to take fresh body prints from living subjects at regular intervals, remember – they can't impersonate anyone without them.'

Martha nodded. 'At least they'll be easier to spot, I suppose.'

'Doctor! Miss Jones!' Lord Haleston was hurrying down the drive towards them, Romand keeping pace just behind him. 'We've been observing the battle. Miss Jones, I'm so pleased you are safe and well. And Doctor – you acted most valiantly.'

The Doctor didn't respond.

'Yes, well,' Haleston went on. 'I must attend to my wife and my friends in the aftermath, take stock of the damage… There will be so much to do…' He hurried away down the drive.

'It was a battle beyond belief,' Romand declared. 'A highly accomplished operation…'

'Operation!' Martha echoed, her heart leaping into her throat. 'Oh god, Doctor, that's right – the Skarasen.'

'What?'

'It's being operated on right now! Taro or some—'

'What?!'

'It's only supposed to take a few hours.'

'WHAT? As little as that?' The Doctor grabbed hold of Martha's shoulders. 'Taro's gonna find that her crew's been wiped out, her dreams are in tatters...'

Martha nodded. 'And I'm guessing once the Skarasen's back under her control, getting him housetrained isn't the first thing she'll do.'

'We've got to get to Wolvenlath,' said the Doctor. 'As fast as possible. *En vitesse! Schnell, schnell!*'

'Whatever are you talking about?' Romand sighed. 'Can't we enjoy a simple victory?'

'There was nothing to enjoy here today,' snapped the Doctor, as he sprinted away down the drive. 'And the cavalry may have won this battle, but the war's not over yet!'

TWENTY-ONE

Martha shivered as the Opel roared along the winding country lanes. She wished the sun would rise faster. The drive through the dawn was freezing cold, and the thought of what lay ahead for them in Wolvenlath was not exactly one to warm the heart. Even the Doctor was taking no pleasure in the drive now. His expression was stern, his movements to control their course precise and economical.

She wished there had been more time to stay and help tend the wounded, assembled on the devastated lawns of Goldspur. Victor and Ian were lending a hand clearing up in the gruesome aftermath, Dr Fenchurch had been duly summoned, and medicinal brandy was doing the rounds ahead of his arrival. Haleston and the cavalry seemed to have things under control. She only hoped the same couldn't be said for Taro the Zygon, over at Wolvenlath.

'Haleston would have posted police guards at the site, wouldn't he?' said Martha.

'I can see one in the road,' said the Doctor.

A sick feeling built in Martha's stomach as the Doctor slowed down in the car. Two more policemen were lying on the grassy verge by the side of the road. One was sprawled on his back, his face a swollen mess.

The Doctor's fists tightened round the wheel as he steered them off the road towards the dirt track.

'What are you doing?' Martha asked as the car bumped over the uneven ground.

'Quick way down,' the Doctor informed her.

The gradient grew steeper, and the car lurched as a tyre burst. 'Victor's going to kill you,' Martha told him, 'if you don't kill us first.' Brambles scraped on metal as the rear of the car caught the hedgerow. As she glanced over her shoulder to see, she caught movement beneath the blanket abandoned in the foot well.

A short muzzle and dark, hazel eyes pushed out from the blanket.

'Teazel?' Martha exclaimed. 'Where did you spring from?'

The Doctor's eyes widened. 'I left Teazel in Kelmore. That must be—'

With a terrifying growl, Teazel jumped up at Martha, his jaws snapping. She cried out, nearly tumbled from the car as it skidded round a hairpin bend. The Mastiff forced its way into the front seat between them, its front legs gashed open and bloody teeth tearing at the Doctor's coat.

'It's a Zygon,' she yelled. The car swerved from side to side as he fought to keep control. Martha hooked her arm around the fake Teazel's neck, tried to drag it off the Doctor's arm. The car smashed over a rock and the wheel with the punctured tyre went flying. The Opel tipped crazily to the left. Martha screamed as the animal's bulk slammed into her. But the Doctor grabbed hold of her wrist, stopped her from falling out, even as the car slithered and span and gouged a crazy path through the gorse and heather.

The dog's jaws snapped at Martha's face. Then, a red haze began to engulf Teazel, and his body began to crack and swell. An inhuman voice slurred out: 'Body... print... *failing*...'

'I set the real Teazel free hours ago,' the Doctor shouted. 'The template's wiped itself from the synthetic circuit!'

Unable to hold on with its morphing hands, the creature fell and hit the ground. A few moments later, the car sideswiped a tree. Martha was thrown against the Doctor and clutched on to him, the heavy thrum of the engine rocking through her like her heartbeat as she gingerly tested her arms and legs for damage. Martha couldn't quite believe she was still alive, let alone uninjured.

Then she heard a guttural, hissing roar behind her,

and turned. Teazel had gone; it was Brelarn who was running down the churned-up hillside towards them.

'Come on,' the Doctor snapped, taking her hand as he climbed out of the rattling car. She jumped down beside him and they sprinted through the wet grass towards the chained Skarasen, lying beside its dead companion.

'It's still asleep,' she panted as they approached. 'That's good, right?'

One giant eye snapped open as they approached, fixed on them.

'OK, maybe not so good,' Martha conceded.

The Doctor changed course, getting out of the Skarasen's sight by running behind its head. The monster roared, and the compacted earth around its buried arms began to shake. Martha was knocked to the ground, and as she scrambled up the Doctor took hold of her shoulders.

'Do you have any idea where the augmented activator and the sonic screwdriver might have ended up?' he asked her urgently. 'Quick! Think!'

'I...' Martha frowned. 'I think your double had them when he went for me in Lord Haleston's hut.'

'Go and see. I'll hold off Brelarn.' The sound of harsh, laboured breathing was getting louder. 'If we're gonna stand a chance of controlling the Skarasen we need—'

With a broiling hiss of anger, the Zygon Warlord appeared from behind the Skarasen's head and rushed to the attack. The Doctor managed to shove Martha clear even as he went down beneath Brelarn's orange bulk. 'Quick as you can!' he yelled.

Martha forced herself to keep running, driving herself faster and faster. Behind her, the wounded Zygon's bellow of rage mingled with the grating roar of the Skarasen, gathering itself to rise.

The Doctor struggled in Brelarn's grip. He saw the barbs in the Zygon's palms, beady with venom, as they moved inexorably towards his face.

Then the Skarasen stirred and shifted and the ground about it shook. At the same time, the Doctor arched his back, breaking Brelarn's grip and knocking him clear. The Zygon cracked his huge skull against a rock and lay still.

The Doctor scrambled up, saw Brelarn was still breathing – then shot a worried look at the Skarasen. It was trying to raise its head, and the heavy chains that secured its neck were pulling taut. He started to run after Martha. But as he passed the abandoned ditch-digger, the squat, red-orange figure of a Zygon scuttled out from behind it, raising her claw-like hands as she blocked his way.

'Ah, Taro, there you are,' said the Doctor, acting casual as he moved a little to the right, blocking Brelarn's body from view. He smiled. 'What's wrong? It's me, Felic!'

'Felic?' Taro hesitated. 'You were supposed to stay here and assist me. What has happened?'

'I encountered some humans. But I dealt with them.' He smiled tightly. 'Have you made the repairs?'

'The healing transmissions were accepted and our control matrix re-established.' She gestured frantically beyond the Skarasen. 'But that vibration in the air...'

'It's the engine of a human motor car I borrowed...' The Doctor shrugged. 'I left it running. Primitive machinery takes so long to start—'

'Silence it,' snarled Taro. 'The diastellic therapy has left the Skarasen sensitive to vibration. You can see it is disturbed. Aggressive thought impulses may weaken the control matrix.'

'Might they now,' mused the Doctor.

As if on cue, the Skarasen roared again. The Doctor jumped as the chains at its neck fell away, clanking and clanging as they tumbled to the ground.

And he saw that Brelarn was back on his feet.

'Uh-oh,' he said.

'Kill the Doctor, Taro!' the Warlord screamed. 'Kill him!'

Taro's face scrunched up in rage. '*Doctor?*'

'What?' the Doctor protested. 'Fair's fair, Felic pretended to be me—'

Taro grabbed for the Doctor's neck. Her fingers caught his flesh and the sting shocked through him. Gasping with pain, he sank to his knees. Then a shadow fell over him as the Skarasen's head blotted out the sun.

* * *

Martha slammed back the bolts on the hut door and threw it open. The hot, iron stench of blood filled the little room; the Zygon body still lay prone in the corner. She covered her mouth with one hand as she knelt down to begin a frantic search on the muddy, bloody floor.

Hang on, she thought, turning back to the body. *That thing's still here. If it's dead, isn't it meant to disappear?*

'It's all right,' she told herself, clearing away a litter of papers and leather-bound books. 'Just means there's no one on the Zygon ship left to spirit Felic's body away. That's a good thing. That's—'

Suddenly the corpse rolled over and lunged for Martha's legs. She cried out, tried to crawl clear, but a gnarled hand closed on her ankle. *Déjà vu*, Martha thought. She managed to yank herself free but over-balanced and fell on the floor. When she tried to scramble back up, Felic grabbed hold of her hair.

'You left me for dead,' the Zygon slurred, leaning in close to her face. 'I will leave you the same…'

He shoved Martha into the shelves that lined the wall and she cried out, collapsing to the floor in a pile of ink bottles and blotters. 'You don't want to kill me,' she told him shakily. 'Your plan's shot to hell – the King's safe and your crew is dead. The only one who can help you now is the Doctor, and if you kill me—'

'You are lying,' panted Felic. 'The Doctor is our prisoner.'

Martha shook her head. 'Try taking his form, then.'

The Zygon clenched its fists, closed its eyes as if concentrating. Martha tried scrabbling up, but Felic opened his eyes again and kicked her back against the wall.

'Can't do it, can you?' she said quietly, clutching her ribs. 'Because he's gone. Face it, you've lost.'

Felic's breathing grew more laboured as he tried again to will the change. The effort made him stagger back and slump against the opposite wall. His dark red eyes opened and stared hatefully into hers.

Suddenly a loud, terrifying roar shook the hut. 'The Skarasen,' Felic whispered, struggling to rise. Martha started to get up too, leaning heavily on a shelf for support. But as she did, something toppled down from a higher shelf to land between her and Felic.

She stared. It was the sonic screwdriver and the activator. The Zygon must have hidden them up there before attempting to deal with her.

Felic grabbed for the fallen prizes just as she did. Martha got the screwdriver, but the Zygon beat her to the activator.

'Give that to me,' Martha shouted.

'No, human.' Felic looked up at her, clasping the activator to his knobbly chest. 'I am dying. But you will never… have control… of the Skarasen…'

So saying, the Zygon ripped away the metal components from the gnarled growth. A rush of red energy crackled round his fingers and sent a spasm through Felic's body. Then he fell backwards, crushing the pieces against the floor with the last of his strength.

'No!' Martha shouted as another wild roar tore through the hut. She snatched what was left of the activator from Felic's lifeless fingers, then threw open the door and ran outside.

To find the Doctor was in deep, deep trouble.

'Die, Doctor,' hissed Taro, her grip tightening on his throat. 'No human can survive the full power of a Zygon's sting.'

'You're forgetting, Taro,' the Doctor gasped. 'I'm – *not* – human!' Bringing up both arms, he broke her grip and pushed her away, then staggered back to his feet. His neck was swollen and burning. He could feel the alien toxins bubbling beneath the surface, sapping his strength. And now Brelarn was coming at him again.

Gritting his teeth, the Doctor stumbled away, circled round behind the ditch-digger.

The Skarasen was properly awake now, and getting angry. The ground quaked as it started to shift one of its buried paws.

'The engine noise must be silenced, Commander,' Taro shouted. 'It is imperative!'

'Go then,' Brelarn hissed. 'I shall deal with this one.'

'Doctor!' yelled Martha. He turned to find her running down the slope towards him, waving the sonic in one hand, clutching something else in the other. The sight of her gave him strength and he staggered to join her.

'Oh my god, your throat…' Martha looked shocked as he approached. 'Are you all right?'

'Adam's apple?' he croaked, reaching for the sonic. 'Overrated. Did you find the activator?'

She pulled a face. 'Yeah, but it's a bit broken.'

He grabbed it from her, held the sonic to it and buzzed. 'No residual delta waves,' he muttered. 'Now it's just a regular signalling device.' He threw it away. 'We can't send the Skarasen back to sleep.'

Martha grabbed hold of his arm. 'Company again.'

Brelarn was slowly approaching, his scarred, hideous features twisted in a gloating smile. 'You have lost, Doctor. With the Skarasen returned to our control, we have a fresh source of food.' The Skarasen roared again as if to underline the point, and the noisy grind of the Opel's engine cut dead. 'We shall rest and recover,' the Warlord went on. 'My children will grow old and strong and thirsty for human blood. There will be other opportunities and we shall take them. Eventually, we shall subjugate this world.'

The Doctor held his ground and shook his head. 'I'll stop you, Brelarn. Wherever and whenever you strike, I'll stop you.'

A ghastly hiss escaped the Zygon's lips as it reached out its blood-soaked arms to him. 'You will be *dead*…'

TWENTY-TWO

As Brelarn lumbered forwards, a gunshot echoed out. The ground spat shards in the air, peppering the Zygon's feet. The Doctor jumped back into Martha's arms, and Brelarn turned angrily to face this new threat.

'Romand!' Martha cried.

The Frenchman was crouched inside the ditch-digger, waving a duelling pistol. He fired again. The shot whistled past Brelarn's head and almost hit Martha. 'Run, you two!' he cried.

'Who from, him or you?' Martha complained, grabbing the Doctor's hand and pulling him towards the shelter of a nearby crane. Brelarn made to follow them, but another whistling gunshot hit a boulder beside him and drove him back.

'Nice shooting, Romand,' the Doctor called hoarsely. 'You've got him on the run.'

'I am trying to hit him,' the Frenchman retorted. 'Damned things, the other one wouldn't hold still for us either…'

'Who's "us"?' Martha yelled.

But the Doctor had already seen Victor and Ian. They were making tracks for the cover of a primitive bulldozer, dwarfed by the Skarasen as it slowly raised its massive paw from beneath tons of soil and sand. Now the engine had cut out, it seemed calmer, but its strength and power were still breathtaking.

Romand spared the giant creature a nervous glance, then fired again at Brelarn. The Warlord was still retreating. He could get away, the Doctor realised, like Taro had got away. And with the Skarasen, he could make good on his threats to devastate the world…

The Doctor jumped up, cleared his burning throat. 'Romand!' he shouted. 'Switch on the engine of that digger!'

The Frenchman looked baffled. 'What?'

'And Martha, you must get this thing started. Starter button's the big one on the right.'

'But why—?'

'Do it, both of you!' He climbed out onto the roof of the crane cab and signalled to Victor and Ian with his arms. They waved back and he cupped his hands to his mouth. 'Engines on!' he bawled, his throat raw. 'Every machine here, anything with a motor, *switch it on!*'

The last of his words were lost in a sputtering roar

as Martha fired up the crane's engine. Romand's digger rumbled into life too, the vibrations nearly knocking the Frenchman clear as filthy steam poured from its funnel.

The Skarasen threw back its head and let rip with a roar that managed to all but drown out the chorus of engines. But Victor had got the bulldozer started, and Ian was already racing to another digger.

'You're making it angrier,' Martha shouted.

The Doctor swung himself back down into the cab. 'We can't let the Skarasen get back under Zygon control. It's healed now, it won't be dangerous of its own free will...'

The Skarasen opened its jaws and plunged towards Romand's digger. He jumped down, dropping the gun, and ran for the cover of the crane as giant teeth tore into the steel framework.

Martha stared at the Doctor. 'Not dangerous?'

'It's just extra-sensitive right now,' he shouted back, patting the crane's controls. 'The engines make vibrations, right? Nasty *sonic* vibrations, disrupting all those sensitive diastellic commands... and hopefully disrupting the Zygon control matrix before it can take full effect.'

Just then, Romand pitched up, panting for breath, and Martha helped him inside. 'What is he talking about?'

'He's giving that thing a brainstorm and hoping the sun comes out again afterwards,' Martha translated.

Romand shook his head wearily.

The Doctor looked up at the angry Skarasen. 'I'm sorry,' he said. 'I'm so sorry, this pain won't last long. You've already thrown off the real chains, now try to throw off the mental ones too…'

'I don't think it's listening,' Martha shouted, as the Skarasen's head snaked out towards their crane. She grabbed the Doctor and Romand by the hand and pulled them both from the cab. 'Jump!'

They all three landed awkwardly together and fell to the ground. The Doctor stared in wonder as the whole crane was mashed up inside the creature's jaws, as the wheels were spat out like pips.

Ian and Victor had abandoned their own vehicles, no doubt figuring they were likely next targets. But without the threat of bullets, Brelarn had ventured back out from hiding. He marched towards them, clutching something in his gnarled hands.

It was the activator.

'You will calm the Skarasen, Doctor,' he proclaimed, raising it aloft, 'with your own ingenious device.'

'I can't,' the Doctor snapped, helping Martha to her feet. 'That thing's useless now.'

'Do it,' Brelarn insisted. 'Or I shall go from here and slaughter all humans I encounter. Females. Infants—'

'It doesn't work! Without my modifications it's just a simple transmitter…' Suddenly the Doctor realised the Skarasen had stopped roaring. Its eyes seemed fixed on Brelarn. 'And it's transmitting now on the recall frequency! Get rid of it, Brelarn. Chuck it away!'

'You cannot deceive me!' the Zygon thundered, holding the activator aloft.

The Skarasen's hideous head darted down, drooling jaws open wide.

'No!' screamed Brelarn. He dived clear of the Skarasen's teeth, rolled over and scrambled back up, raised his hand ready to hurl away the activator...

But the Beast of Westmorland would not be denied. Its teeth closed on Brelarn's arm. The Zygon Warlord screamed as the Skarasen's head lifted back up into the pale morning sky, taking him with it. Then the scream choked away, and the great jaws twitched as they chewed.

'Good God,' cried Victor, as he and Ian came running up. 'It ate him!'

'It ate the signal device,' the Doctor corrected him. 'Brelarn just happened to be attached.'

'From Warlord of the Zygons to Breakfast of the Skarasen...' Martha turned to Romand, Ian and Victor. 'Good to see you. But what are you lot even doing here?'

'We realised Brelarn was missing from the dead and wounded at Goldspur,' Ian told her breathlessly.

'Yeah, noticed, thanks,' said the Doctor, his eyes still riveted to the Skarasen.

'We came in Mr Romand's motor car to warn you,'

Victor added. 'And I couldn't help but notice my *own* car was—'

'Not now, Victor.' The Doctor was staring up at the Skarasen, willing it on. 'Come on... come on, my beauty...' It roared again, and stared down at the lakeshore. 'You're confused, I know, you're not sure what's going on. You've eaten that duff old activator 'cause you thought you had to, but now with your control matrix kaput, nothing's coming through, nothing's screaming at you. Free will. Doesn't it feel good?' He nodded, encouragingly. 'And then you look down and you see, right at your feet...'

'A dead Skarasen,' said Martha.

Romand nodded. 'Its own kind, no?'

'And to any animal,' said Victor, 'such a sight spells danger!'

'A Skarasen isn't "any animal",' the Doctor said softly. 'So the question is, does it know how to spell at all...?'

Abruptly the Skarasen backed away from the corpse on the lakeshore, splashing out into the depths of the lake. Then it turned and submerged, its enormous neck and head crashing beneath the surface. A few moments later, the huge, beached corpse of its twin lurched, scraping against the shingle as it was dragged deeper into the lake.

Ian stared. 'It's taking the dead one with it.'

'Its place is in the water now,' murmured the Doctor. 'Not here.'

The charred, broken head of the dead Skarasen dipped beneath the shiny grey surface of the lake. The water churned and seethed for a few moments. Then, all was calm.

'Well.' The Doctor slowly puffed out a long breath. 'What a clever boy: Beast of Westmorland spelling test, ten out of ten!' He smiled round at Victor, Ian, Romand and Martha. 'And B-Y-E spells *See-ya, Skarasen!*'

'And G-O-O-D riddance!' Martha laughed.

'Has it really gone?' Ian marvelled. 'Gone for good?'

'For good? It's gone for *brilliant!*' the Doctor told him. 'There's a subterranean channel leading out into the Irish Sea. The Skarasen will find its way to freedom. That's lovely. Isn't that lovely?' He glanced over at the digger and the 'dozer, whose engines were still rumbling away. 'But that racket's ruining what ought to be a very promising morning.'

'I'll turn them off,' said Ian, happily running to oblige.

'I've already switched off the Opel's engine,' said Victor sadly. 'What's left of it. I hadn't realised you—'

'Sorry, Victor.' Martha was pointing, her face grave. Everyone looked. With the Skarasens gone, they could see straight across to where Victor's car lay smashed against the tree.

Taro was crawling past the wreck of the motor car, forcing herself up the hillside.

'Thought I'd killed the thing,' said Romand coldly.

'With the same pistol they were ready to turn on the King.'

'Wait here,' said the Doctor, striding off purposefully towards the injured Zygon. 'All of you. I'll be back.'

'Doctor!' Martha called, but he didn't look round.

'Shall we go after him?' Victor wondered.

'No.' Martha shook her head a fraction. 'Give him a minute.'

Taro wasn't moving fast, she couldn't. The Doctor soon caught up with her. He could see she was bleeding from her side. As he approached, she hissed, tried to crawl a little faster.

He stood a few metres away from her. 'Is that wound serious?'

She lay still, panting for breath. 'You will kill me before I can die from it.'

'Will I?' He walked over and sat beside her, just out of reach. 'Why would I do that, then?'

'Why would you not?'

'Because you're not all the same. And because I know you've lost just about everything.' The Doctor looked towards Martha and the others, back in the valley, and sighed. 'I hope none of them ever find out what that feels like.'

The distant drone of the machinery died. An eerie silence settled over the valley.

Taro's brows were knitted together in a fierce frown.

'I do not seek your pity, Doctor.'

'That's good, 'cause I've got none to give,' the Doctor retorted. 'Just a proposition to put to you. Go back to your ship, summon your surviving crew, wherever they might be, and rejoin the children. I checked your relays, you've got enough power left for a single trip. Leave here, hide yourselves and return to the amber. Sleep.'

Taro hissed weakly. 'To await a rescue that may never come?'

He came closer. 'It's the best I can do.'

Taro grabbed his hand in hers. 'Your body is weakened by my venom,' she croaked. 'A further sting…' She looked up at him. 'I could kill you.'

'And then my friends would kill *you*,' he said evenly, not resisting. 'Your crewmates would starve to death, and your children would have no one.' He looked her in the eyes. 'I won't give you a second chance, Taro.'

Slowly, with a wheezing breath, she let go of his hand and turned away. The Doctor sat beside her in silence as the minutes passed, as the sun climbed slowly into the sky.

From the field beside the TARDIS, Martha surveyed the majestic sunset. The red sun sat low in the sky, reducing the rugged landscape to a series of sharp black shadows. And a dark, spidery spaceship was whizzing by high overhead, the whine of its drive systems devastating the silence. She looked round at the select audience who'd gathered here besides her and the Doctor – Victor, Romand, Ian and Lord Haleston. They held their hands over their ears, staring as the ship slowly dwindled into the pink sky.

'No more Zygons, then,' she murmured. 'They're really leaving.'

'Somewhere nice and remote,' the Doctor agreed. 'North Pole? Or the South Pole. Somewhere polar, anyway.'

'We should have killed the lot of them,' said Lord Haleston darkly.

The Doctor sighed. 'That's right, your lordship, end the day on a smile.'

'*I* certainly shall,' Ian informed them. 'Nanny Flock has taken to her bed. Nerves and bruises, Dr Fenchurch says. He's given her a tonic.' He grinned nastily. 'And *I've* swapped it for cod liver oil.'

Romand laughed. 'A taste of her own medicine, yes?'

Haleston cleared his throat. 'A little respect and decorum, if you please, gentlemen.'

'You won't tell Mother and Father, will you, sir?' Ian asked, wide-eyed. 'I should hate to set back their recovery.'

'He'll be far too busy helping out with the recovery of my motor car,' said Victor, smiling at Haleston. 'Won't you, old buck?'

'Yes, sorry about your car,' said Martha. 'You're insured though, yeah?'

He looked at her blankly. 'Insured?'

The Doctor lowered his voice. 'No proper car insurance till the 1930s.'

'Ah,' said Martha. 'Unlucky.'

'On the contrary,' said Victor. 'After living through all that has happened here, I feel as lucky a man as the King himself.'

'As do we all,' Haleston suggested, 'for playing our small part in protecting the life of the monarch.'

'Long live King Edward,' cried Ian, and Martha joined in the chorus of agreement.

The Doctor nodded. 'Though why he was named after a potato will always be a mystery to me.'

Haleston's face darkened, and Martha hid her smile by turning towards the TARDIS. She thought of all the people who'd be coming home just as they were leaving. Little Molly, reunited with her family. Ian's parents back together with Teazel. The real Mrs Unswick, taking back ownership of her Lodge. And poor Clara, who'd be visiting her parents' church for a final time. Martha was still wearing the girl's cardigan. She wanted to bring it out into the stars with her; a little piece of the girl she'd never known, that would fly forever.

'I take it,' said Lord Haleston, his grave voice interrupting her thoughts, 'that you have some luggage stowed away in this extraordinary object?'

'Lots,' Martha agreed. 'We'll just go and get it.'

Romand took her hand and kissed it. 'And then, my dear, it will be my privilege to run you to the station in my motor car, yes?'

'If my own car wasn't in pieces, I'd offer the same service myself,' said Victor, pressing a kiss against her other hand.

Martha smiled at them both. 'And if I was going to the station, boys, I'd take you up on it.'

Ian looked puzzled. 'Then, how are you getting home?'

Martha smiled round at them all one last time, as the Doctor unlocked the TARDIS door and slipped inside.

'Don't let appearances deceive you,' she said, giving Ian's hand a fond squeeze. 'This *is* our home.'

Ian watched her follow the Doctor into the strange-looking police box and close the door. Victor and Romand frowned at each other, and Lord Haleston started to mutter something about inappropriate behaviour under his breath.

But then, a groaning, grating sound started up, and a strange breeze with it. The light upon the police box began to flash. Slowly, the entire box faded from view. Everyone was left staring at the square of flattened grass left in the box's wake.

Lord Haleston's face twitched as he struggled valiantly to keep calm. 'Preposterous,' he squeaked at last. 'How dare the wretched man! There *must* be an order to the world, a proper place for everything! Dear, oh dear…' He turned and bustled away, muttering under his breath.

'Impossible,' breathed Victor.

'Indeed,' Romand agreed. 'And yet I think, perhaps, for the Doctor and Miss Jones, the impossible *is* their proper place.'

'That's for certain.' Ian grinned. 'Happy travels, Doctor, Martha. The more impossible, the better!'

Acknowledgements

The author would like to thank everyone whose care and contribution have enhanced this book. In particular Justin Richards and Gary Russell (green lights, guidance and encouragement); Steve Tribe (extra editorial input); Philippa Milnes-Smith (special agent); Linda Chapman (equine advice and support); Paul Magrs, Mike Tucker and Jason Loborik (sanity-saving); Russell T Davies and Robert Banks Stewart (obviously); Terrance Dicks (for *Doctor Who and the Loch Ness Monster*); and not forgetting Jill and Tobey Cole (patience, kindness and fun).

Also available from BBC Books
featuring the Doctor and Rose
as played by Christopher Eccleston and Billie Piper:

DOCTOR·WHO

THE CLOCKWISE MAN
by Justin Richards

THE MONSTERS INSIDE
by Stephen Cole

WINNER TAKES ALL
by Jacqueline Rayner

THE DEVIANT STRAIN
by Justin Richards

ONLY HUMAN
by Gareth Roberts

THE STEALERS OF DREAMS
by Steve Lyons

Also available from BBC Books
featuring the Doctor and Martha
as played by David Tennant and Freema Agyeman:

The Last Dodo

by Jacqueline Rayner

ISBN 978 1 84607 224 6

UK £6.99 US $11.99/$14.99 CDN

The Doctor and Martha go in search of a real live dodo,
and are transported by the TARDIS to the mysterious
Museum of the Last Ones. There, in the Earth section,
they discover every extinct creature up to the present
day, all still alive and in suspended animation.

Preservation is the museum's only job – collecting
the last of every endangered species from all over the
universe. But exhibits are going missing…

Can the Doctor solve the mystery before the museum's
curator adds the last of the Time Lords to her collection?

Wooden Heart

by Martin Day

ISBN 978 1 84607 226 0

UK £6.99 US $11.99/$14.99 CDN

A vast starship, seemingly deserted and spinning slowly in the void of deep space. Martha and the Doctor explore this drifting tomb, and discover that they may not be alone after all…

Who survived the disaster that overcame the rest of the crew? What continues to power the vessel? And why has a stretch of wooded countryside suddenly appeared in the middle of the craft?

As the Doctor and Martha journey through the forest, they find a mysterious, fogbound village – a village traumatised by missing children and prophecies of its own destruction.

The Inside Story

by Gary Russell

ISBN 978 0 56348 649 7

£14.99

In March 2005, a 900-year-old alien in a police public call box made a triumphant return to our television screens. *The Inside Story* takes us behind the scenes to find out how the series was commissioned, made and brought into the twenty-first century. Gary Russell has talked extensively to everyone involved in the show, from the Tenth Doctor himself, David Tennant, and executive producer Russell T Davies, to the people normally hidden inside monster suits or behind cameras. Everyone has an interesting story to tell.

The result is the definitive account of how the new *Doctor Who* was created. With exclusive access to design drawings, backstage photographs, costume designs and other previously unpublished pictures, *The Inside Story* covers the making of all twenty-six episodes of Series One and Two, plus the Christmas specials, as well as an exclusive look ahead to the third series.